THE TRUTH BEHIND THE LIE

ALSO BY SARA LÖVESTAM

Wonderful Feels Like This

THE TRUTH BEHIND THE LIE

Sara Lövestam

Translated by Laura A. Wideburg

MINOTAUR
BOOKS
NEW YORK

First published in the United States by Minotaur Books, an imprint of St. Martin's Publishing Group

THE TRUTH BEHIND THE LIE. Copyright © 2019 by Sara Lövestam. All rights reserved. Printed in the United States of America. For information, address St. Martin's Publishing Group, 120 Broadway, New York, NY 10271.

Translation copyright © 2019 by Laura A. Wideburg

www.minotaurbooks.com

Designed by Omar Chapa

Library of Congress Cataloging-in-Publication Data is available upon request.

ISBN 978-1-250-30007-2 (hardcover)
ISBN 978-1-250-30008-9 (ebook)

Our books may be purchased in bulk for promotional, educational, or business use. Please contact your local bookseller or the Macmillan Corporate and Premium Sales Department at 1-800-221-7945, extension 5442, or by email at MacmillanSpecialMarkets@macmillan.com.

First published in Sweden in 2019 by Piratförlaget

First U.S. Edition: August 2019

10 9 8 7 6 5 4 3 2 1

THE TRUTH BEHIND THE LIE

PROLOGUE

The rain was so strange the day they took Julia. Tiny drops, a heavy mist almost, but slowly and imperceptibly, you still got soaking wet. Julia noticed it, too:

"Look at the rain, Mamma! It's not really falling. It's like those tiny mosquitos; what are they called, Mamma?"

She turned her face up to me, her tiny nose damp, and her hood fell off her head for the fifteenth time in a row. I pulled it back on, not all that lovingly and tenderly, as I think back, and I took her hand.

"Are you thinking of no-see-ums? Come on, now, Julia, we're going to be late."

She wrangled her hand out of mine. She was stubborn that way. IS. She IS stubborn.

"Oh, right, no-see-ums."

I've thought back on those words so often. The last words I heard from my daughter:

"Oh, right, no-see-ums."

As if they could give me a clue.

CHAPTER 1

Private detective. If the police can't help, call me!

Kouplan isn't sure if he should have mentioned the police. He knows how words work. Any police officer reading his ad would get stuck on the word *police* and that could bring unwanted attention. On the other hand, he needed to reach the right kind of clients. Now his ad is up on the same website as all the ads for cheap, really cheap, and super cheap cleaning services. It's been up for two weeks now and not a bite.

His e-mail address is a regular Hotmail address, like thousands of others, and not connected to any other place on the net. He's certain it can't be traced. Nobody can come knocking on his door unexpectedly.

He'd found the computer in the trash room of his apartment complex. It worked just fine. It had an old operating system and hardly any memory. A week later, he found a monitor in the same trash. Its only fault was that it weighed

a ton and had the resolution from the Windows NT era.
When he connected it and started the computer, a box
popped up and told him the hard drive was full. It seemed
there were hundreds of photos of a few neighbors from the
other end of the apartment complex. Every once in a while,
he'd glance at them. Today he just wants to find out if anyone answered his ad.

> Hi Kouplan! Thanks for your message. I'm fine. So are the
> kids. How are you doing? Are things starting to work out? The
> lawyers didn't have anything new for me, but I promise (as
> you know) to get in touch as soon as I find out anything use-
> ful. Right away. Take care now and love from me! Karin

He stares at his message for a while and wonders if
he should answer now or later. "Are things starting to work
out?" Well, now, that all depends on what you mean by
that. He clicks the next mail.

> Saw your ad. Need your help right away to find my little girl
> who disappeared last Monday, near the Globe Arena Center.
> Can't call the police. Will pay well.

Pay well? Kouplan would have leapt at it even if just
the word *pay* had appeared. As he searches her name, he
thinks he would like to believe he'd help even if she didn't
have any money. A missing child. His mom lost a child
once. Actually, twice.

•   •   •

He Googles her name and e-mail. On her Facebook page, she looks blond and average, some office worker, and has thirty-two friends. She works in telephone support, it appears, and he doesn't detect any hint of an undercover policewoman. He types a reply:

> Hi, Pernilla. I'm a private detective. I have worked on kidnappings among other things. Give me your number and I'll be in contact. I can help you.

He realizes he's shaking. Walking around in Stockholm would be the stupidest thing he could do, given who he is. Stockholm, a city where people walk through the city with their bags of groceries and talk breezily into their smartphones about their fish pedicures and Princess Estelle. A city where every corner can be dangerous and anyone could dig their claws into you, like a harpy, and demand your soul.

On the other hand, from now on he will be the detective. He's the one who will be spying on others, not the person spied on, or whatever the word for that could be. He'd be one with the shadows.

CHAPTER 2

Pernilla has noticed that she's been re-washing clean mugs ever since Julia disappeared. Rubbing invisible stains on the stove, working late into the evening to avoid hearing the silence, the water running through the pipes. Julia's absence is a vacuum, a deadly gas, if she lets it inside. So she dusts the clean shelves one more time and holds on to whatever keeps her busy. Reads all the papers, looks for clues, takes out money from the bank in case they want a ransom. She searches online under "girl found" and has gone back hundreds of times to the place where Julia pulled her hand away, but she hasn't contacted the authorities, for her own, very specific reasons. That private detective mentioned situations where the police can't help. That's what gave her the courage to contact him.

She's dusting when her phone pings, shattering the silence. The sound makes her jump. She's put her phone on the highest volume, so she wouldn't miss a call in case it was Julia, or someone who found Julia. Now, she slides her finger along the screen, opens the message, hopes. It is the private detective and his last sentence holds her heart like a parachute. *I can help you.*

The detective with nothing more than a Hotmail address wants her phone number. Her dog Janus is ready to pee on himself. He's whining and giving small barks as he stands by the door. A dog's bladder does not care whether or not someone has disappeared.

There are so many *ifs*. If they hadn't decided to go shopping at the Globe Arena Center on that very day. If she had held on tighter to Julia's hand. If there hadn't been so many people around. If they'd at least taken Janus with them.

Janus pees on his favorite post. When he's done, Pernilla raises her voice into an eager falsetto.

"Janus! Find Julia!"

Janus wags his tail.

"Janus! Where's Julia?"

She tries to make it sound like a game, but her voice breaks. *Where is Julia? Is she even alive?*

Janus wags his tail and looks around, confused. Pernilla squats down and buries her face in his fuzzy coat.

"It's all right," she murmurs into his soft ear. "You wouldn't know."

They say mothers can tell by instinct if their children are alive or dead, but the more she tries to feel her instincts, the less she can differentiate her instincts from her desires. Finally, she shoves the thought away. She can't leave that gateway open. She's holding hard to the leash with one hand, her telephone with the other.

Thirty seconds after she sends her number, her phone rings.

Kouplan isn't sure what he should expect, but he's still surprised by how small her voice sounds. You can cry your eyes out—can you cry your voice out? Pernilla's voice isn't loud, but she has an obvious Stockholm dialect, and he makes his first-ever mental note as a detective:

She's from here. A native.

She asks what he thinks.

"One website said that if a child has been missing for more than a week, it's probably . . . it's probably too late. Is it? Is it really too late?"

He hasn't studied the subject, but he knows that answering questions has one purpose: to create trust.

"Each case is different," he says with his most Swedish accent. "There are always exceptions and there's always a way."

"She hasn't been gone for a week yet," the voice in his ear says. "Not even a week. It's only the fourth day."

"I see," Kouplan says, because there's nothing to say when another person is trying to find some hope.

"I don't want to call the police, but Missing Persons say they won't do anything until I've given them a statement."

The woman on the other end does not hear Kouplan sigh in relief.

"No, we won't bring them in," he says. "We should meet tomorrow morning, early, at the place where she disappeared. What was her name again?"

For a brief moment, he thinks that she's hung up. Then her voice returns, tinier than ever.

"Julia."

Kouplan notes it. Then he has to take up that other piece of business.

"Well, the mon . . . the commission."

"I've read up on that kind of thing and know it's seven hundred Swedish crowns an hour, more or less."

Seven hundred an hour? When he worked at a restaurant, he was lucky to get fifteen an hour. Mostly it was twelve. *Seven hundred?* Did he hear that right?

"I'm only going to take four hundred an hour, but I'd like some of it in advance, if that's okay."

Pernilla informs him that she's aware that an advance is customary. Kouplan writes down the number in the notebook he'd gotten at his Swedish as a Second Language class. *Julia, 400, the Globe Arena Center.*

Before he goes to bed, he writes down a plan. It's the first time he's written a real plan since he's come here. A real plan for real work, that is, a plan he's learned how to make from people who knew more than he did. During the evening, he searches the Internet, through the papers and telegram offices, the uncensored forum Flashback, and the latest updated information from web pages with all the words he's put on his list. When he finally hits the sack, it's past three in the morning and his eyes can no longer focus. For the first time in a long time, he falls asleep immediately.

CHAPTER 3

Kouplan has a peculiar relationship with his heart. He's training it. He's the coach of his own heart, and he commands it to slow down. Just like doing really good push-ups: slow and controlled, stopping an inch above the floor before slowly coming back up. His heart has to be beating slowly so he will seem like a bored commuter.

The girl across from him believes the new iPhone comes in both black and white. She's insisting she's seen it in an ad. She blasts the information right into her iPhone 4S.

"Okay, sure, do you have a copy of Metro? It's that ad, I swear! And there was a white one in the picture, but . . . yes, the iPhone! . . . Jesus, can you just listen to me? It's important!"

Behind the girl there's a group of gangly teenagers, and leaning against a seat, a woman who could be a police officer. She's got that straight neck police officers get and she's letting her gaze wander over the other passengers.

Kouplan puts his elbow against the window and looks out over Årstavik Bay, as if he is unbelievably bored, and, above all, relaxed.

The girl in the seat across from him is calling someone else to confirm that the iPhone does come in white. He can hear the person on the other end say she should check on the net. "Yeah."

Kouplan gets up, and keeping the erect figure of the policewoman at the edge of his vision, exits through the other door. His heart follows his orders.

He walks over the bridge to the Globe Arena Center as if he were a completely ordinary man. It's not Pernilla's fault she lost her kid here, he tells himself. Still, he would have preferred any other place to this one. The rubber soles on his shoes suck up water from the wet asphalt, but from the top, they look good. His jacket is in worse shape. He found out that people look at the jacket first, then the shoes. Oh, well. It's early in the morning and nothing is going on. Just people on their way to work. He's on his way to work, too. He just has to project that feeling.

Pernilla doesn't know what to expect. Obviously not a Sherlock with a pipe, a trench coat, and a magnifying glass. She's not that naïve. Perhaps it's that black-haired guy with a briefcase walking quickly past her, who stops and stares into a display window, perhaps to study her from her reflection. Perhaps it's that hipster riding by on a bike. He gets off and locks it to a tree. He takes off his helmet and runs his hand through his more than unruly head of hair.

It could be him, even if he's now heading right into the mall and is gone from sight. Certainly it can't be that teen-age kid in washed-out jeans, who stops in front of her with a questioning look.

"Pernilla?" She nods, confused, and takes the hand he's holding out toward her. From his eyes he appears to be, perhaps not fourteen, as she'd first guessed, but hardly more than eighteen. He smiles as he presses her hand.

"Let's sit down, shall we?"

As they start to search through the Globe Arena Center for a place to sit, she makes up her mind not to give him any advance. At least, not until she's questioned him thoroughly.

"I can barely stand being in this place," she says in spite of herself, because he's the only person she can talk to. "Even though I've been here many times since last Monday, it makes me feel ill. I don't know what I'm looking for, and my dog Janus is not exactly a bloodhound. I don't know . . ."

She lets her sentence hang in the air.

The boy detective gestures toward McDonald's.

"It looks empty in the corner. Let's sit down."

Kouplan has many favorite Swedish expressions. One is "truth with modification." It's a kind of truth that is not all that true. For instance: *Size doesn't matter.* Or: *The eyes are a window to the soul.* If eyes really were windows to the soul, Pernilla would not be looking at him with such skepticism. She would have realized at once that she was dealing with a sharp man who had the competence to solve her problem.

"I'm older than I appear," he says and catches her eye.

It is a truth. Pernilla smiles in embarrassment, as if she suspected this but didn't dare ask.

"I'm twenty-eight," Kouplan continues.

That's a modified truth. Still, adding three years to his age is not a sin.

Pernilla's eyes narrow, as if she doesn't believe him.

"It's a genetic issue: My genes make me look younger."

That is a truth, and Pernilla can tell. She smiles quickly.

"You could make a fortune if you figured out how to sell that mutation."

"I just wanted to put that out there, because I know you had to be wondering about it," Kouplan says.

Pernilla straightens her back, clears her throat.

She hasn't touched her cheeseburger.

"Before we enter into a contract, I need to know more about you."

Kouplan takes a bite of his burger. It tastes better than the ones you buy and bring home on the bus in a paper bag.

"Shoot," he says.

"How long have you worked as a detective?"

"To tell the truth," Kouplan says (and here comes another modified truth), "I've only worked as a detective for the past year. Before that I did investigative reporting. So, basically, I was trained as a journalist."

Some old Nazi once said that if you want people to believe a lie, make it a big lie. But Kouplan knows better than to trust a Nazi slogan. He tells truths and modified truths, and when Pernilla asks about his career in journalism, he can answer.

"I have a great deal of experience in kidnapping," he says.

That is a truth.

Pernilla begins to sniffle once they leave the restaurant. She's about to show him where it happened, but she can't get a word out. He lays a hand on her shoulder and feels her body stiffen.

"So you were walking here," he says in a calm way, as if talking to a frightened child.

Pernilla nods.

"In this direction?"

She shakes off his hand and vaguely gestures toward the entrance to the mall.

"That way."

"What brought you here?"

"We were shopping. Julia needs new winter shoes. And also I needed to buy groceries."

Kouplan writes this down in his book.

"Are you absolutely sure this was the spot?"

He takes out his cell phone and begins to take pictures in every direction.

"The people we see can see us," he explains. He feels uncomfortable hearing his own words out loud. "All the people in the restaurant, for example. Was it crowded when it happened?"

Was it crowded? Pernilla doesn't remember. The more she tries, the less she can remember. She and Julia, in that rain she could barely feel. She sighs, shudders, tries to give this man-boy real answers.

"It was raining, but not hard. Almost misting."

He writes in his book that looks to her like one of those composition books from elementary school.

"Did you have an umbrella?"

He's looking at her in such a demanding way that she doesn't tell him what she really wants to say. *What does it matter whether or not we had umbrellas? Find my daughter!*

"No, our faces were getting wet. But Julia had a raincoat, in bright pink."

Again she can feel the rain landing on their faces with the wind against them. The detective writes down that Julia was wearing a raincoat.

"Did anyone else around you have an umbrella?"

She nods.

"Some people did."

She remembers it now, because she remembers thinking that their umbrellas weren't much help with rain hanging in the air like it did.

"About three or four people walking in front of us. And one person covered her head with a Metro newspaper."

"And?"

"She was probably worried about her hair. I think she went into Subway or that Greek place."

"Did you notice anyone looking at you? Anyone who slowed down? Anyone who came and went and came back again?"

She closes her eyes and tries to see the umbrellas in front of her. In her memory, they're all dark, either dark blue or green, and they are heading in the same direction as they were. The next moment, Julia's hand slips out of hers.

"No."

At Subway, a lone girl is working, wearing an apron and with her hair in a bun.

"Can we sit down here for a minute?" asks Kouplan, and the girl squints at him with a touch of suspicion.

"Only if you buy something."

Kouplan looks at Pernilla, who looks back at him perplexed. He can't afford to buy even a single sandwich.

At last, Pernilla says, "Half a turkey sandwich and a coffee with milk."

"Coming up," the girl says, and turns to the sandwich board.

Most kidnapped children are taken by one of the parents. One of the things Kouplan had read last night, on many of the sites he'd visited. He hoped that Pernilla's ex was a real bastard who'd been sneaking after them and took her away, because the other alternatives he'd found had been more troubling: extortion, adoption, child labor, murder. He asks about Julia's father, but Pernilla shakes her head.

"His name is Patrick. Go ahead and write it down if you want, but I doubt if he has anything to do with this. He ran off after Julia was born and I haven't heard from him since. I've never even asked him for child support."

Even though she's shaking her head, Kouplan asks for Patrick's last name. Otherwise he wouldn't really be earning his four hundred an hour.

"Hey there," the girl behind the counter says. "Your turkey sub is ready."

As the girl hands them the turkey sandwich, she gives him an obligatory smile. Kouplan smiles back.

"Were you working here last Monday?"

"What do you mean?" She looks at him suspiciously.

He must smile more broadly.

"Nothing about you, but I was wondering if you saw a little girl. About so high, wearing a bright pink raincoat. Was she here on Monday?"

She wrinkles her brow.

"No, why? Why are you asking?"

"We're looking for her."

She looks at him as if she doesn't understand what he's talking about.

"Is she missing?"

The bell on the door rings, and a new customer enters

and orders a large sub with extra garlic dressing. Kouplan writes a few numbers on a napkin.

"This is my cell phone. Call me if you remember anything."

The girl's mouth drops open.

"Are you a policeman?"

The new customer turns and stares at Kouplan. It happens so quickly that he doesn't have time to control his heart: It starts to pound and his legs are ready to run. He stops them by willpower alone and manages to shake his head.

"No, the police don't get involved in custody . . . things. Custody matters. So we're trying to find her ourselves."

Pernilla has gotten up. She casts a glance at the new customer, then looks at Kouplan and the girl, who seems more interested.

"That's right," she says. "The girl is my daughter."

Kouplan realizes what an idiotic case he's agreed to take on. As soon as he asks if someone has seen a missing little girl, he'll be finding himself talking about the police. Then people will call the police. The police will start hearing rumors and they're going to start wondering why a dark-skinned man, with a blue jacket and brown shoes, is doing their work. He'll have to think of something better to say.

"We're trying to find her father. He has her now, but he's moved to an unknown address, that bastard."

It works. The girl's eagerness disappears. The question

of a girl in a pink raincoat is now uninteresting. The new customer leans over the counter.

"Do you have any roast beef?"

Kouplan knows why the entire world is his enemy. He knows why he has to travel cautiously like Jum-Jum in the Country of Faraway, why anyone could be one of knight Kato's soldiers. But why Pernilla doesn't want to report this to the police is something she hasn't told him.

"Have you had a bad experience with the police?" he asks when they head back out onto Arenavägen again.

"With the authorities," she replies.

Kouplan nods. "Me, too."

Pernilla places a bundle of hundred-crown notes in his hand.

"I'll need a record of your time and exactly what you've done."

"That's fine."

"And your name."

He hesitates, but what can be more suspicious than a guy with more than one name?

"Kouplan. K-o-u plus plan."

Pernilla looks him right in the eye. Her own are tired, blue, and belong to someone who must have already turned forty. Cried-out eyes.

"Here you go, Kouplan," she says and hands him the turkey sandwich, uneaten and still wrapped in its paper. "You're looking a little thin."

CHAPTER 4

All at once, Julia decided she wanted a dog.

"Ohhh," she started to say whenever we looked at cute pictures of dogs on Facebook or met dog owners in the city. My shy kid, who hardly says her name to other kids or adults, becomes fearless; she can run right up to a mastiff or a poodle—my daughter doesn't discriminate—and begs me to let her pet it. "Can I pet him?" she'd ask me and not the owner, and I'd smile.

"Ask the owner, not me," I'd say, but I knew she wouldn't dare. I'd ask, "May she pet your dog?"

Sometimes it worked, sometimes it didn't. We probably pet fifty dogs that spring, and by the time her sixth birthday rolled around, I'd decided.

"I'm not bringing you your present in bed," I declared at breakfast.

Julia looked up at me, a whipped-cream mustache above her mouth because we always celebrated our birthdays with hot chocolate.

The accusation on her face, oh, my little rejected six-year-old. And then, her happiness when she realized what was going to happen instead.

"The dog shelter?"

I patted her head and smoothed out some knots in her hair before I kissed her on the forehead.

"It's a place for dogs who have no owners. You can go pick out a dog there, if you really want a dog."

Screams of joy.

I was the one who taught her to be skeptical of other adults, so I really can't say that her true nature is shy. "Some people you can trust," I said, whenever we brought it up. And she learned to repeat after me. "And some you can't." I hope that she learned which ones were those you can't trust and I hope that she pulled away and ran for her life. When they took her.

The first dog she saw at the shelter was Janus. He was a shaggy mixed-breed dog as tall as her waist and he had a happy manner that started in his eyes and went all the way to the tip of his tail.

"Oh, Mamma!"

I still can see her enraptured face, her light freckles, the way she couldn't take her eyes from Janus. Even though the dog was still called Challe then. But on the way home, you could see the change in him, how his posture straightened and how calm his curly coat became. He left the shelter as Challe, an ownerless mixed-breed dog, but he got off the bus as Janus, the dog belonging to the Svensson family.

"Why Janus?" I asked as we rode up the elevator.

Julia grimaced in that way she had, as she does have, when she's trying to pull something over on you. She peers through one eye and pulls in her mouth; something is going on inside her original, unique mind.

"Because we were in a shelter and Jesus took shelter in a manger, but we can't really call him Jesus, can we?"

I laughed and then Julia laughed, too. The elevator arrived and Janus sniffed at what would become his floor.

"All right then," Julia declared in her inimitable voice as I unlocked our door, "now we have a dog!"

You know how you can feel a certain kind of calm that shows just how stressed you've been? I felt more secure after we got Janus. He wasn't the biggest dog in the world, and he never got angry, but he's a dog with a sensitive nose and sharp teeth. In the evening, when my big six-year-old had fallen asleep in her bed and I was sitting up in front of the television, Janus would come and put his head on my lap. His loyalty crashed over me like a wave. If anything were to happen to Julia, or me, he would come to our defense. Our brave soldier. That's when I realized how scared I had been.

CHAPTER 5

Kouplan eats his breakfast either before seven or after eight a.m. He ought to eat with the family, that's what the family says, but he never feels like it. He feels like an intruder, or like they would start to take an interest in him. At five to eight, the mother heads off with both the children, and he waits five more minutes before he opens the door between his space and theirs. He usually stretches his legs then, because their floor space is so much larger than his. He jogs in place and then he does three rounds of pushups and walks around the apartment while his porridge heats up in the microwave. He keeps the lights off, even though it's started to be dark in the mornings. In just a few months, it will be as dark as coal, and so will the room.

Before he leaves the apartment today, he puts two hundred crowns on the table with a note. *More later,* he prints with a style of handwriting he calls Mister Neutral. They used to use one like this in the newsroom back in the

day, a handwriting so standardized that it couldn't be identified as belonging to a specific person. He learned to do
the same thing with the Swedish alphabet by studying the
posters in the children's section at the library. *You can
never be too careful,* his brother used to say. Unfortunately,
his brother was right about that.

At eight thirty, he uses both keys to lock the door to the
family's house and notes the time in his notebook. Should
travel time be part of a detective's paid hours? He'll have
to do an Internet search on that later, as it wouldn't be professional to ask his customer what to include in his bill.

Before he leaves the stairwell, he opens his mouth as
wide as possible, then brings his teeth together, opens his
mouth again, takes a deep breath, and walks out as a free
human being. And wealthy.

"Youth?" the cashier asks at the kiosk where he's buying his transit card. She scrutinizes him more carefully
than necessary.

A youth card costs three hundred crowns less than the
transit card for adults. You can save a small fortune. However, you have to show your ID to prove your age to any
ticket checkers.

"Adult," Kouplan replies as the pang of losing three
hundred Swedish crowns burns his stomach.

The beep and the green arrow as he pulls his card
through is a relief, an embrace of welcome. Citizen, you
are allowed onto the subway! Congratulations!

Behind him, three or four guys are waiting to sneak

through the turnstile. For the next month, he won't be one of them.

According to Pernilla, Julia's father was not behind the child's disappearance. Still, you can't ignore statistics, so Kouplan changes at Västra Skogen station and takes the subway to Sundbyberg. The best outcome would be never to have to go back to the Globe Arena, ever.

Patrick Magnusson, the man who never cared about his daughter, works as a freelance accountant. Kouplan found that out just by looking through LinkedIn. On Facebook, he found that the man likes history and through Eniro, the Swedish public tax registry, that he lived with someone named M. Siegrist in a house not far from Sundbyberg's center. At the house next door, there is an older lady who keeps nude stone angels in her garden. Kouplan can see her blurry figure through the window. Her hair sits like a yellowish white feather duster on top of her head.

When he rings the bell, she opens the door right away.

"Hello?" she says as she flutters her eyelashes.

"Hi," Kouplan says and makes his body language into a teenager's. "I'm from Björke School and we're collecting money for a math field trip."

She laughs.

"A math field trip? And what are you selling?"

He smiles his broadest smile and thinks about how easily fourteen-year-olds get embarrassed.

"Nothing, we're just collecting bottles we can return

for the deposit. So if you want to get rid of some bottles, or some aluminum cans . . ."

The collecting bottles for deposit idea was number one on a list he made called *2A: Reasons to ring the bell at people's houses.*

The older lady studies him and tries to figure out if he is a criminal by his appearance.

"Why don't you wait here?" she says.

He waits. After a minute, when she still hasn't returned (how long does it take to find a couple of bottles anyway?), Kouplan's thinking speeds up. *Perhaps she's called the police? Does he look like a burglar? How many break-ins have there been in Sundbyberg lately?* He should have checked that! The largest angel in the garden is aiming its bow and arrow right at him.

"Here you go! Not many, but I hope it helps!"

He swallows. If he is going to go into this profession, he can't suspect people of calling the police all the time. He just can't.

"Thanks so much. It will really help."

She starts to shut the door, but he clears his throat and smiles again.

"I'm just wondering if I should go this way or that."

"How so?"

He winks at her: That often works on women, even those close to sixty.

"Who do you think has the most bottles?"

By the blond woman's answer, he can conclude that

the Magnusson-Siegrists are not big beer drinkers and
that they don't have any teenagers in the family, either.

"Not smaller kids? Or, perhaps, a relative's kid?"

She laughs and looks at him strangely. He's gone
too far.

"It's getting chilly," she says as she closes the door.

Since the older woman is keeping an eye on him, he decides to hit the other neighbors before he rings Patrick
Magnusson's door. By then, Kouplan has three full bags
of believability.

"I'm from Björke School," he says in his fourteen-year-
old voice. "We're collecting bottles to return to get money
for a math field trip."

Patrick studies him. Patrick is one head taller and he's
blond. Kouplan tries to imagine him with Pernilla. They'd
be a real Aryan laundry detergent commercial.

"Björke School?"

Kouplan should have checked the names of schools
around Sundbyberg before he left. He'd read the name
Björke School in a book.

"Yeah," he says.

He peeks into the hall. Adult shoes in two prim rows.
An empty dresser and a classic statue with two faces. No
children's shoes, not even a coat hook. No traces of children
anywhere. No spills, no mud.

"A math trip," he says quickly. "A field trip where we
get to do math problems all day. Different subjects. We're
going to Berlin if we get enough money."

Kouplan smiles with his sorry-to-disturb-you look, not the charming look for ladies over sixty.

"Otherwise, we're going to Uppsala."

Patrick lets him wait in the hall, not outside. *Trusts people*, Kouplan writes in his notebook. If he stands next to the statue, he can almost see all the way into the kitchen. A narrow vase for flowers balances on a similarly narrow pedestal by the window. In a family with children, like the one he's staying with, that'd be just asking for trouble.

He gets five green Carlsberg Hof bottles from Pernilla's former husband, and two plastic bottles of Loka flavored water. He hasn't gotten any new information, but at least he'd get nine Swedish crowns in bottles out of it.

The digital display on the bottle-return machine puts him in high spirits. Sixty-four, sixty-five, sixty-six—the numbers keep ticking up and he still has three bags to go. After Patrick's house, he kept going down the entire street—because he's not an idiot—and he found out that people drink a great deal of beer in Sundbyberg. As he starts to put the bottles from the last bag into the machine, he sees someone grinning at him.

"Good day, huh?" says the slightly smelly Grin, and Kouplan nods, pleased with the nickname he has chosen.

Kouplan, bottle collector. It's been a long time since he looked down on himself for doing this, but he still has to remind himself that he's no longer that person. He is working undercover.

"Two more and I'd have enough for half an Explorer," the Grin says with jealousy.

Kouplan gives him two cans and gets a musty blast of bad breath in thanks.

"Nice of you. You guys are nice, in spite of what people say."

Kouplan doesn't bother to reply. Still, as the Grin beside him puts in his bottles for money halfway to what he needs for his bottle of Explorer vodka, he starts to think. *Who are the people who know where other people disappear?*

"By the way," he says and acts like one of the Grin's other pals. "Do you know of a little girl that has gone missing?"

The Grin shakes his head, and his grin disappears.

"Nah, damn. Sorry, don't know what you're talking about."

He has 260 crowns in his pocket and he feels rich. He stops at Lidl and buys three packages of oatmeal and five cans of crushed tomatoes for ninety-eight crowns. Then he asks where he can find the nearest secondhand store. It's the only place he'd ever find a decent jacket for under five hundred crowns.

The problem is that it has to fit and it has to be the right kind. Especially not too big. If it's too big, he might as well just keep using the one he already has. Finally he finds one that fits and makes him look like a normal guy in the wintertime. It costs 350 crowns.

He holds on to it for a while, keeping it under his arm as he pretends to look at other things. A copper kettle, porcelain dishes with lids. Finally, he studies the cashier and the two people who are walking around putting things away, folding and rehanging clothes that people tried on. The cashier is someone he can't ask. She looks irritated and the way she holds herself signals she is responsible for the economics of the shop. The other girl seems young, not over eighteen, and probably can't make any independent decisions. So the third one looks promising. Especially when considering her pierced lip.

"Excuse me."

She looks up, gazing intently. She's cut her hair short on one side and has light-colored dreadlocks on the other side of her head.

"This jacket," he says and looks her right in the eyes. "It says three hundred and fifty crowns and I only have one hundred and thirty-eight."

She nods. "Then I guess you have to choose another one."

She smiles in a friendly way and turns back to hanging up clothes.

"But I need this one," Kouplan says. "I can't tell you why, exactly . . . but this is the one I need. And when I say I only have one hundred and thirty-eight crowns, I really mean that's all I have."

The girl turns back to him. Looks at the torn summer jacket he's wearing. It looks like he found it in a garbage can. Actually he *had* found it in a garbage can. He opens his plastic bag.

"See? This is all the food I have. I don't have any money, really, but I need this jacket. Please . . ."

His ex once told him Swedes don't like pleading, but he was desperate.

"Well, this jacket," the girl with her dreadlocks and lip piercing says, "this one has been priced wrong. It should be fifty crowns. I'll re-tag it and bring it to the counter for you."

At that exact moment, she is the most beautiful person he's ever met.

CHAPTER 6

The Grin with his beer cans sticks with Kouplan all night long. He dreams that the old alcoholic stacks cans one on top of the other, then starts climbing them so he can touch the clouds. *Who are the people who know where missing people are?* he says, slurring his words. His beer-drenched breath turns into Carlsberg-green dragons that swim out into the atmosphere and fall back to earth. He wakes up at five. *Who are the people who know where the missing people are?*

The people who know the answer to that won't be at that fast food place before ten in the morning, so Kouplan spends his morning searching the Internet. *5:46 a.m.*, he writes into his notebook. *Research on human smuggling.* On the web, a human smuggler is defined as an individual who helps foreigners enter Sweden, the EU, Iceland, Norway, and Switzerland illegally. They keep mentioning Amir

Heidari. On the English web pages, there's nothing on either Sweden or Switzerland. But they say there's a difference between human smuggling and human trafficking. Smugglers work with the people they sneak in, but not trafficking. He changes his search words.

06:12 a.m. Research on human trafficking.

First and foremost, women and children are affected, he reads. He makes a note of this. Women and children are lured from poor countries to rich ones, from the countryside to the city, in order to work in households or factories. He writes down main points in his notebook. He underlines the most important phrases.

Half of trafficked people are children. Children are kidnapped for <u>adoption</u>. Seven reports of <u>sexual human trafficking</u> in 2010 were cases concerning <u>children. Prostitution, trade in human organs,</u> child soldiers, <u>forced labor.</u>

Kouplan thinks that forced service as a child soldier would be an unlikely outcome for six-year-old girls. Adoption or prostitution would be the most logical choices. He puts his hand out over the floor, estimates in the air about how tall she would be. Then he regrets doing it. He doesn't want to think of her as a child.

When he gets to the grill, he feels ill. He's been training his stomach like he's been training his heart: just focus on digesting the breakfast oatmeal. Nobody remembers me here. They forgot to look me in the eye.

He sits down at the table closest to the kitchen entrance and orders a kebab with bread, even though his stomach is doing somersaults with the oatmeal. Azad looks at him emptily, looks through him, and asks, "Anything else?"

Kouplan doesn't say, *Hey, it's me, remember?* Instead, he says, "No onions, please."

This way, Azad will remember that it was some Swede in his restaurant at ten in the morning, should anyone ask. Swedes never put onions on their kebabs.

Ismet cuts the kebab from the slab of meat hanging next to the wall. Azad asks a few girls in cloth jackets if they want anything on their falafel. "No onions, please," they say as Kouplan sticks out his foot. The swinging door opens and Rashid is standing inside.

"Rashid!"

He whispers at first, but realizes it's better to yell. The girls at the counter are busy wondering whether or not they want to add hummus.

"Rashid!"

Rashid jumps. *Is that how frightened he used to look when he didn't expect people to call out his name?* He has to realize he's taking a big risk.

"*Negaran nabash,*" Kouplan says. *Don't worry.*

Rashid wrinkles his brow. Studies Kouplan, comes closer to look at him better.

"Nes . . ."

"Shhh!"

"Is it really you?"

Kouplan shakes his head. "No, it's not me."

He smiles and Rashid laughs out loud. Actually, it's really good to see him again.

"I've got to work."

"I have cigarettes."

"Give me two minutes and go round the back."

The backside of the restaurant smells like frying oil and something rotten. The odor is as strong as a childhood memory, from that time when he was the one who cleaned the oily grill on the other side of the wall. Rashid laughs again when he sees Kouplan through a crack in the door. He has a warm look, still, but his laugh is short as if he has to save it.

"Nice to have visitors," he says.

"I wonder if you can check something for me," Kouplan says as he hands over the cigarette pack, which quickly disappears into Rashid's pocket. "Just ask around for me."

The good thing with Rashid is that you don't have to explain things to him. He just repeats what Kouplan tells him.

"Six years old," he says. "I'll ask the people I live with."

Kouplan doesn't explain why he came to Rashid. Rashid knows. People who know where missing people might be happen to be people who have disappeared themselves.

"Don't say a word about meeting me," Kouplan says again, just to make sure.

More like a statement. He has an inspiration and pulls a fifty-crown bill from his pocket. He'll be getting four hundred Swedish crowns from Pernilla for the time he spent at the grill.

Rashid takes the money without blinking.

Kouplan starts missing him as soon as Rashid shuts the door.

He remembers an Iranian proverb after he's left the grill. *Cho istadei, daste oftade gir* vibrates through him like a song he can't stop listening to. *As long as you are standing, hold out a hand to those who have fallen.* Since he's standing and Rashid has fallen, it feels good to give him some money. *Cho istadei, daste oftade gir.* The proverb reminds him who he'd been. Someone who doesn't collect bottles.

Pernilla is sitting with Julia's pajamas in her hand. It's Sunday. Julia disappeared last Monday. Janus is walking around her, wagging his tail. He puts his head protectively on her lap. The weight of his head makes the pair of pajamas seem even emptier.

"She's not here, Janus."

Where is she? Janus's eyes are asking.

"I don't know. Nobody knows."

He scratches, crawls up onto her lap. He's a family dog, he can figure out when a person is feeling low. Brought to the pound because of an allergy. He smells the pajamas, puts his head right on top of them. His warm body is trying to tell her something, but she can't take it in. She can't cry now.

"I'm going to call Kouplan."

His high voice is like a teenager's, but it still helps her calm down. There's something comforting in him, something that comes from parents who cared and from an experienced soul. Pernilla has nothing like it, and she knows something basic in her is missing, because that's what she's been told. Still, she tries to be a good person, and she was a good mother. *Is* a good mother. Kouplan is telling her that he's talked to a few colleagues to get tips and has also gone to see Patrick. *Patrick? Why would he have seen Patrick?*

"I told you he had nothing to do with it," she reminds him with irritation.

"I'm using established methods," Kouplan says in his mature teenaged voice. "I have to eliminate close relatives to make progress in . . . the case."

She thinks she's heard the same thing on Criminal Case, so he's probably doing the right thing. Or perhaps he heard the same thing on Criminal Case. At any rate, Kouplan had gone to Patrick's.

"So, how's he doing?" she asks in the most disinterested way she can.

"Well . . ."

"Remember, I'm the one paying you," she says with a smile she hopes can be heard through the connection.

"It seems he's doing well, from what I saw."

"Is he still living in Bromma?"

"No, he moved to Sundbyberg with a girl. Or maybe a guy, who knows. There were two names on the mailbox at any rate. They own a Volvo."

She hesitates asking, as it gives her a lump in her throat. But the question comes anyway:

"Any children?"

"Nope."

A cushion, like a cloud, lightens her heart.

She is so relieved that she wants to sing, despite her current desperate situation. She'd always wondered if he'd gone on to have children with someone else. Maybe many children. She'd dreamed he had, and those had been nightmares.

"He didn't like children," she says. "So it's probably for the best."

"What do you mean?"

"What?"

"What do you mean, he didn't like children? Did he do something to Julia?"

"You mean hurt her?"

She had to think. She and Julia had lived with the emptiness of a father who had left; they'd both cried through the night. Sometimes together.

"He didn't give a damn about me or her from day one. Besides that, no."

Kouplan is silent, but he is present. She can hear his presence through the connection. She is also silent.

"I'm going to see another old colleague," he says. "And tomorrow I'm going back to the Globe Arena. But there's something I need."

"What is it?"

"Can you send me a photo? It's kind of hard to search for someone when you don't know what the person looks like."

Pernilla had been careful with pictures. She'd been careful with everything. Facebook, Eniro, and all the other places where people look for children, and she's not even sure she has a picture of her child, but that would be hard to explain on the phone.

"I'll look for one."

"That would be good."

His voice. As warm as the dog on her lap.

"Come by tomorrow," she listens to her own voice say out loud. "I'm going crazy just sitting and waiting. We can talk."

"All right. Have you eaten today?"

A strange question from a detective. But it's relevant, she realizes. As she gets up, she's dizzy and the pajamas fall to the floor. Janus picks them up with his teeth and as she stumbles into the kitchen, he follows her. The pajamas hang from his muzzle like a lifeless, extremely thin child.

CHAPTER 7

Mondays are the worst. All the apartment doors open to let people out; the dam bursts throughout the city. For every person, there are twice as many eyes; for every eye, a hundred million strokes of a keyboard that can take him in, analyze him, and then run right to their phones to report him, and that's what it looks like when he lets his thoughts go where they will. *I'm just one of them,* he thinks, and he lets his blood circulate more slowly through this body. Be calm my heart; don't use up all your beats before I turn thirty.

He gets off the subway at Gullmarsplan and walks the last bit to the Globe Arena, just as Pernilla and Julia had done exactly one week ago. Mondays are the worst, but in this case it's the best day he has. People with normal lives have normal routines. Those who were here last Monday are probably here today.

•   •   •

The girl at Subway recognizes him. This means she has a good memory for faces, and also that she'd be a good witness, able to identify him if anyone asks. The police had been in the shop.

"I wanted to help," she says as panic spreads into all of Kouplan's limbs.

He can't hear what she says next, because he's doing all he can to keep his body under control. *Calm down, my heart; stay still, my legs and feet—but be ready.*

"They had no idea what I was talking about," she said, shaking her head. "Or maybe they were on their break and didn't want to work."

"Their break?"

"Yeah, they came to buy sandwiches. They didn't know anything about it at any rate."

His fear diminishes, slowly but surely.

"So you didn't *go* to the police."

She looked at him as if he were an idiot.

"No, they were here. Soccer, you know, Hammarby against Djurgården . . ."

He almost had to laugh and tell her that riot police are hardly involved with kidnapping cases. But he shrugs instead.

"As I said, there's no point in bringing the police into it. It's a custody issue and they don't prioritize them."

"Have you found the father yet?"

"Not yet. Thought I'd ask you if you remembered anything. If you saw anyone."

She shakes her head and asks him if he wants to buy

a sub. He thinks back to the turkey sandwich Pernilla had given him. Someday he will go to Subway, order a Spicy Italian with extra pepperoni, nonchalantly slap down a hundred-crown bill and say, "Keep the change."

"No, thanks."

At the Greek restaurant, there are four people working. One of them thinks he has time to talk to Kouplan. He takes a drag on a cigarette and the ends of his mouth turn down in a way that lets Kouplan know he is a real Greek.

"No," he says. "No idea. Yes, lots of kids come through here, especially yesterday when it was AIK against Bajen. Oh, the girl at Subway said Djurgården? There were some guys who wanted to fight, and I'd never take my kids to matches like that. Last Monday? How do you think I would remember anybody who came in here last Monday? Are you out of your mind?"

He doesn't remember any pink raincoat.

"*Efharisto*," Kouplan says, and the man's blank look reveals he's probably not from Greece after all. *Efharisto* is *thank you* in Greek. "Thank you, anyway."

The office of the real estate agent on the other side of the street had windows so squeaky clean that Kouplan didn't want to go in. He also skips a Nordea bank.

At the Thai restaurant, they hadn't seen a little girl that morning.

"What about last week?"

"It go fine."

"What?"

"Bring girl, we have child menu."

The waitress points at a menu. And Kouplan doesn't speak Thai. He tries to wave his hand to indicate last week, not next week.

"Ah!" the woman says, as if she's thought of something.

"Did you see her?"

The waitress shakes her head.

"No, sorry."

Arenagången is the broad pedestrian walkway separating the realtor's office and the Thai restaurant from the Subway and the Greeks. Small trees surrounded by stone walls divide it in two.

If he were going to kidnap a little girl, he'd hide behind one of the stone walls. So he does. It's now 10:23. Julia was kidnapped at ten thirty.

The people walking toward him can be seen easily, even though he's standing behind a tree. If he were taller, the leaves would cover his view, so he sits down on one of the stone walls and glances toward Gullmarsplan subway station. You can sit here and look like a perfectly normal person. Would he appear as normal if it were raining?

He's hit by a thought and he takes out his notebook.

Line of Inquiry 1: Somebody who needs a child.
Line of Inquiry 2: Somebody who knows Julia.

Somebody who wants a child would find a good place and wait. He or she would need a crowd, or a number of people around at the very least. Several good escape routes and a smart way to force or tempt a child to be quiet. The kidnapper could have hidden in one of the restaurants, but not at the bank or at the realtor's. Or perhaps come walking from the opposite direction, from the Globe Arena Center. Escape routes . . . Kouplan looks around. Subway station entrances in three places, but no place to drive a car. At least two hundred meters to each of the station entrances. A stolen child might try to scream or kick. Perhaps the kidnapper drugged her.

If he didn't already know her. Line of Inquiry 2.

If Kouplan had money on his cell phone, he'd text Pernilla. Instead, he writes in his notebook: *Do you usually go to the Globe Arena Center every Monday?* Probably not, he thinks. The girl is six. She probably goes to daycare. This means that any person who wanted to kidnap Julia in particular must have followed mother and daughter, perhaps the entire way from their home. Or perhaps knew that they were going to the Globe Arena that very morning.

He notes down both possibilities. Then he checks out the area around him. Road, stairway, square, center, and, of course, the Globe Arena area itself. Time to widen the search.

He hardly believes a kidnapper would take his victim into a shopping mall. More likely, he would head straight to the subway. The entrance by the arena is the closest.

The kiosk owner down by the platform looks at him

the same way as the girl at the Subway. As if he were a complete idiot.

"A week ago? Look, I have three hundred customers a day! And five hundred are kids, if you get my drift."

Kouplan gets his drift.

"But if there's something unusual going on, perhaps you'd remember it? *Tkaya?*"

The last word is a guess, because the man appears Kurdish to him. The kiosk owner breaks into a grin.

"*Kurdî qise dekeyt?*"

Kouplan grins back. "Just a little."

The kiosk owner likes when people speak a little Kurdish to him. He tells Kouplan of two instances of men carrying a child during the week, three with baby carriages, one mother with short hair and one that was extremely attractive. One child was screaming and kicking, but this was a boy, unfortunately. He doesn't remember any child in a pink raincoat.

Kouplan writes his cell phone number on a receipt someone left behind. One of these days, he'll have shiny business cards with his name embossed.

"*Sipas dekem.*"

The man nods and holds his hand out over the counter. He shakes Kouplan's energetically.

"Good luck!"

Kouplan has nothing when he gets onto the bus to Pernilla's house. No witnesses, no clues, no leads, nothing. Can he really be paid for nothing? All he has is four questions he's written in pencil. He steps off the bus and looks around the neighborhood. A little reconnaissance. How does a woman live whose child has gone missing?

CHAPTER 8

A woman whose child has gone missing can live in a rental apartment building with green balconies. This one has the code 1111. He enters it and takes the elevator up. It smells clean. If he ever had a child, he hopes he or she would be able to ride in an elevator this clean every day.

Pernilla looks smaller than the first time they met. In his memory, she was about the same height as he was, but she's almost five feet, six inches. She's put her blond hair into a ponytail. She smiles, her face is pale. She asks him to come in. A sandy-colored and very happy dog pushes past her calves. Kouplan keeps his reflexes under control and lets the dog sniff his crotch.

Pernilla has painted her hallway white, except for one wall, which is blue. Beneath the clothes hangers, there are two hooks at the right height for a child. A child's jacket hangs on one. It has a shiny surface. He wants to ask if it's new, but decides to be considerate and lets the question rest. On the shoe rack, there are rubber boots in kids' size eight and a half. He glances around the properly cleaned apartment as Pernilla clears her throat.

"It's a little messy," she apologizes.

"It looks great."

"Coffee?"

Kouplan sits on her sofa, which is a light mocha color and has a lighter stain on one of the arms. He's looking at the stain; certainly she's noticed it.

"It was a ketchup stain," she says.

Her stomach knots as she thinks about it. Everything, absolutely everything here, reminds her of Julia. Kouplan looks at her in confusion.

"What?"

"Ketchup made that stain. I thought you were looking at it."

His eyes follow her gesture and he studies the arm of the sofa, as if he has just noticed the stain that moment.

"I had no idea that ketchup makes light stains," he says.

"Neither did I. It's because it's acidic, I think. Julia spilled a whole bowl of macaroni right there, but it was a while ago."

He concentrates on her, this boy who is actually a man. Not suspiciously, but with attention. She realizes that he's going to start asking her questions.

• • •

Kouplan sees immediately that he is invading a space now empty due to a missing child and that Pernilla is desperately trying to fill it with normal gestures and words.

Only the dog seems unaffected by what's going on. He trots through the apartment with his own agenda.

"So, I wrote down everything," he says as he opens his notebook. "Here you go. Interview with a waitress, a kiosk owner, a Greek restaurant owner, reconnaissance of the area . . ."

He doesn't know if she will pay now or later and what kinds of rules apply to this situation, but since he's living outside the rules anyway, it will have to depend on the situation.

"Okay, that's good," she says and leans over to see what he's written down. "What have you found out? Can we ask for any recordings from security cameras or something like that?"

"Only the police are allowed to view those," he says, and he believes that to be the case. "One thing we do know is that nobody in the area noticed anything unusual. I know it sounds like . . . there's not much information. But it's good that at least we know this. I'm going to keep interviewing people until we find which direction he went. If she didn't . . ."

He hesitates; he was about to say *if she didn't go willingly.*

"I have two main theories," he says instead. "The first

is she was picked at random. The other is that it was Julia, herself, they were after."

Pernilla swallows and takes a deep breath. He can see her focus.

"All right."

"So I thought we could make a list of why anyone would want to take Julia."

"All right."

The thought of a list of why someone would want to take Julia feels like the kind of dream you have right before you fall asleep. A dream where you can't stop falling, where your heart thinks you are going to die and your hands grab for the mattress. Pernilla holds onto the edge of the sofa and the knuckles of her fingers turn white.

"No detail is too small," Kouplan says.

"She's very well-behaved."

Kouplan writes.

"So you think she might not resist a kidnapper?"

She tries to imagine Julia in front of her, fighting a stranger with her tiny arms.

"No, but she's easily frightened, she's easily frightened and a little unusual."

Unusual, Kouplan writes.

"What do you mean by that?"

"She has an odd sense of humor. She's kind of subtle, if you can say that about a six-year-old."

He nods.

"Have you noticed any adult show more interest in

her than seems normal? At her daycare . . . or a playground?"

She has to think. *Where would Julia meet adults?*

"I don't send her to daycare," she says. "I work from
home, in telephone support, so she's never needed to be in
daycare or preschool. Perhaps if she'd been a more active
child, but she's fairly calm. Perhaps . . . the library. We go
to the library sometimes."

"All right, let's start with the library. Is there anyone
in particular who would talk to Julia? Start a conversation
with her?"

Pernilla pictures in her mind the people working at
the library. The one with short hair and glasses. The white-
haired one with the corduroy jacket. They always greet
them in a friendly way when she and Julia come in to ask
whether a certain Alfons book has been checked out or
not. They like Julia. They like all the kids who read. But
start a conversation with her . . .

"No, nothing beyond normal."

They go through all the places she and Julia used to go.
The shops, the playgrounds, the toyshop. Then it hits her.

"Could this be why they'd take her? As opposed to
someone else?"

"Because?"

"Because she's so quiet and careful . . . because she
doesn't make a lot of noise. If they wanted someone
like . . ."

She takes a deep breath to be able to say out loud what
has come to her mind.

"A girl like Natascha Kampusch, the girl they kept in a basement. They wanted a nice . . . a nice . . ."

She can't keep control over her body any longer. She lets go of the edge of the sofa. She falls.

When Pernilla faints, he thinks for a moment that she's dying, but realizes in a split second that she's fainted; the air is shimmering as if an electric current has gone through it. Then the dog jumps onto her lap, barking, and Kouplan gets up and goes to the kitchen and gets some water. The cup is a plastic one with Mickey Mouse on it. The water sloshes as he walks back, and the dog is licking Pernilla's face and when her eyes begin to move behind her lids, both he and the dog can release their breath. He gives her the water.

"I'm sorry," she says.

Her shoulders are so lonely, he thinks. Her back, her neck, her longing. She needs a hug, but probably not from her detective; he has no idea how she'd take that. He sends a silent thank-you to the sandy-colored, warm body of a dog, who is now lying across her legs.

"How are you feeling?" he asks.

"I'm fine," she says. "I'm sorry."

She shakes her head and her jaw tenses, two times.

"Time to take a break," she says.

Her eyes see the plastic cup and maybe she wants to say something else, but she keeps it to herself. Her blue eyes get caught in Kouplan's.

"I want my normal life back."

• • •

To give her five more minutes, just to make sure he says that he has to go to the bathroom.

The bathroom is in white and gray and in front of the tub, there's a light-blue shower curtain. He silently opens the bathroom cupboard, and thinks this is part of his legitimate rights as a detective.

Inside, there's a pacifier, a full tube of Idomine salve, three packs of tampons, disinfectant, and panty liners. A prescription of penicillin with her social security number on it. He memorizes it. On the sink, there's a tube of children's toothpaste and in the mug, there's a large and a small toothbrush. He looks at the small one for a minute. It has a dinosaur on the handle. Thinks: *I'd faint, too, if I were her.*

When he comes back into the living room, she's gone.

He stands next to the sofa with its light-colored stain and looks around dumbfounded before he hears banging in the kitchen.

Pernilla doesn't even look up when he walks into the kitchen. She's melting butter in a frying pan.

"Do you like fish sticks?"

Kouplan is fairly sure he likes fish sticks. At any rate, they smell wonderful and start a minor revolution in his stomach and they certainly wouldn't contain any pork. Still, he asks just to be sure. Pernilla stares at him.

"Are you Muslim?"

He shrugs. When is anyone a Muslim?

"So why don't you eat pork?"

Her question might be antagonistic, or might be just a question. He can't tell.

"Why don't you eat dog?" he asks back.

Pernilla makes a face and raises her eyebrows as she flips the fish sticks in a well-practiced way.

"You must really like pigs, then," she says.

"Not all pigs," he replies.

He doesn't like his own joke; it is not right to call people names, not even the police, though they hunt for him all over the city. You have to be above it all.

At any rate, Pernilla smiles.

"Some pigs are easier to love than others, I imagine."

She whisks some powder into water and heats the pot.

"It's mashed potato powder," she says as she glances at him. "I can't make real food right now. I'm making a double portion for you, but you don't have to eat all of it."

He eats all of it. A double portion of powdered mashed potatoes and eight fish sticks. The fish sticks taste vaguely like fish, the potatoes like nothing at all. Still, it fills his stomach until it hurts.

"I can make some dolma for you the next time," he tells her, and smiles as energy spreads through his arms and legs.

"Did you like it?" she asks.

"Yes, it was good," he says and smiles so that she'll believe him.

As she clears off the table, he takes up the questions again. Perhaps it will work better if he asks them in passing.

"A photo of Julia. Did you find one?"

She says nothing, wiping a glass in silence.

Finally she says, "I wish I had more. I wish I were like those crazy moms putting their kids' pictures up on Facebook all the time."

"I only need a few."

"I'll have to look."

He understands by her voice that there might not be any photos. He can tell it's something she regrets. He changes the subject and moves her frying pan to create the illusion he's helping her with the dishes.

"Do you look alike?" he asks.

She smiles at the dishwater.

"We look very much alike. We could stand in front of a mirror together and compare our . . . our noses and our eyes and . . ."

She sniffles, perhaps close to crying.

"We look very much alike," she concludes.

He's ready to leave and she doesn't want to let go of those deep brown eyes. They've kept her thoughts from racing. This boy-man has even got Janus to fall asleep. When he gave her water, he'd put a hand on her shoulder, just for a second or two . . . when he walks out the door, she is going to be all by herself again, with the emptiness that had been filled with Julia. But she doesn't keep him.

"What are you going to do tomorrow?" she asks.

"I'm going back to the Globe Arena," he says. "It's still

possible that someone saw something. I just need to find the right person."

His face looks unchanged from when he was sitting on her sofa, but his eyes begin to flicker and stare and narrow almost imperceptibly as he puts on his jacket. She wouldn't have noticed it if she hadn't recognized it.

"Are you all right?"

He swallows, nods, smiles widely.

"Yeah, I'm great," he says.

But he was not all right. She's thinking about it as she changes into her nightgown. Kouplan is afraid. She didn't notice the first time she met him, just as you don't notice the exact minute your child has gone missing. But after he's sat on her sofa and eaten her fish sticks and showed her in detail how you go about finding a missing child . . . she realizes she's become aware of him as a human being.

She checks the door before she goes to bed. Shudders as she checks the door handle. What if the door flies open and somebody's out there?

"Janus!" she calls in a voice pitched too loud in order to frighten away her own thoughts. "Janus, come sleep in the bed!"

Julia was the one who would creep into her bed whenever Julia had nightmares.

"Nightmare," she'd say as she wedged her scrawny body beneath the blanket.

Pernilla would stroke Julia's hair then and sing to her. Finally, Julia would fall asleep and then Pernilla would fall asleep, too. They'd fall asleep to the sound of each other's breathing.

Janus's breathing is completely different. It's filled with slobber and quick breaths and sometimes he whimpers in his sleep. At least he's breathing.

CHAPTER 9

There's a police car in front of the apartment building where Kouplan lives. It appeared around six in the morning and was still there a little after eight. And still there at nine. At nine-thirty, Kouplan has done one hundred fifty push-ups and sent an e-mail to Karin telling her he now has his transit card. He asks her about an ID card, even if he's fairly sure she can't help with that. She probably doesn't even know that there's someone online named Fletch, who charges two thousand crowns to make a driver's license. She certainly doesn't know that to get a really good driver's license, you have to pay ten times as much. As that thought enters his mind, it swirls like a disturbed nest of wasps so he has to do ten more push-ups. Looks out the window. The police car is still there.

You can't go crazy, his brother said seven years ago. His brother had strong eyes, brave even when he was afraid. Kouplan can still hear the unique sound of his voice and it's saying you can't let the fear eat you alive. *What are we doing here?* his brother says. *Are we shrinking or growing? Focus! What are we doing here?*

Kouplan exclaims the answer he learned seven years ago: *We're working.*

By five past ten he's completed a map of all possible leads, undeveloped lines of inquiry, people who might be interested in Julia. *Time is flying,* he writes in the corner as a reminder. He has to figure out the most important clues and concentrate on them.

When the phone rings, he jumps, not from fear but because his mind had been so focused on his work.

It's Rashid.

"My name is Kouplan now," Kouplan says. "Forget that other name when you call. You should always ask for Kouplan."

"Okay, Kouplan."

"Okay."

"I've asked the guys I'm sharing a place with if they know people involved in human smuggling and they want to know why I asked."

"What did you tell them?"

"I said I was worried about my wife's safety. I needed to know who to keep an eye on."

The people in Rashid's apartment didn't know anything. They'd looked at him as if he were the one who wanted to buy a human being. But then someone dropped by, one of the same guys who got them the job at Azad's grill. And after two glasses of vodka, they started discussing Rashid's question.

"What did you find out?"

"There's this guy, M.B. They don't like him, you can tell by their expressions."

M.B. Kouplan writes this down.

"Just M.B.?"

"He works with girls, trafficking all over Northern Europe, they say. If anyone thought grabbing a child off the street would be a good idea, it'd be him. But that wasn't all."

Kouplan writes. *Northern Europe. Girls.*

"They were talking about *the girl.* All the others were *women,* but one was *the girl.*"

Kouplan shudders, even though he knows hearing this kind of thing will be part of his job. Even though this girl could be anyone, even though he's working. Rashid knows nothing more about this M.B., just that he has a big nose and likes his whiskey. For some reason, the whiskey drinking was supposed to be funny.

"I'm not sure I know why. Maybe because they stick to beer, Azad and the others. I don't know."

"Thanks, Rashid."

"No problem . . . Kouplan."

The police car is still in the street. You have to be rational and logical to keep from thinking that they are waiting for you.

Kouplan goes back to his computer and types in *M B,* in order to start somewhere. He gets megabytes of hits on Mercedes-Benz. *M* and *B* are common initials, perhaps the

most common in Sweden, and a search on Eniro brings
him nothing.

Perhaps M.B. means nothing more than that the man
owns a Mercedes-Benz. He also finds hits on the Medical
Library as well as a song by Orup. When the song starts
buzzing around in his brain, he goes into the kitchen and
makes a pack of noodles.

*Line of Inquiry 1. Someone needs a child. M.B.? Buys
and sells women, "the girl"? Plan: track down an "M.B." in
Rashid's contact network. Ask around the Globe arena about
a man with a big nose.*

*Line of Inquiry 2. Father (Patrick). No traces of a child
in the home. Can be psycho and be hiding child in basement.
Probably not. Plan: Call as if part of a survey and ask if he
has a child (best not from cell phone or home phone).*

*Line of Inquiry 3. Pernilla. Is there something she hasn't
said? Why doesn't she want the police involved? Plan: Ask
about Julia and their life together. Ask why she's avoiding the
police.*

*Line of Inquiry 4. Someone else in Julia's circle of ac-
quaintances. Map out her circle, see Line 3. Plan: Talk to the
employees at the li-*

He hardly has time to react as the children burst
through the door and into the apartment they share.
Regina is on the threshold.

"Hello, Kouplan!"

Kouplan quickly shuts his notebook and smiles apologetically at Regina and tries to smile in a child-friendly way to the kids.

"Just done with my lunch and been sitting around."

Regina laughs. She has a broad mouth.

"I've told you, you're free to be in here."

Kouplan keeps the ends of his mouth turned up, wonders if he can ever look as hearty as Regina. He nods toward the window.

"Something going on?"

"What . . . oh, the police car. No, I have no idea."

"It's been there since six thirty."

"My, that's a long time. . . . Liam! Be nice to Ida, please!"

A screech comes from the living room and Regina hurries away. Liam is apparently not being nice to Ida. Kouplan ought to go back to his room, but stands in the doorway.

"She took it!" Liam is insisting in a loud voice.

Liam is five or six years old. He's just tall enough to look over the kitchen table. He argues volubly with his sister. He drops crumbs on the floor when he eats sandwiches, and has a way of explaining why the candy is missing from the box, and right now he's screaming as if the sky is falling. When he sees Kouplan, he shuts up immediately. His sister grabs the tractor they'd been fighting about and Liam stares at Kouplan with sky-blue eyes.

Kouplan wants to ask him: *If someone came and took you, how would you react?* That would be idiotic, to ask him a question like that in front of his mother. No matter how he tried to ask it, she would notice how strange it was and start paying more attention to him and keep him in her memory more than she needs to.

Kouplan's brother suddenly laughs: *Keep you in her memory? Are you kidding? You already live in her apartment— she's not going to forget who you are!*

Liam's wide eyes are staring at him.

"Did you see the police car?" asks Kouplan, in order to say something.

Liam smiles in the exact same way Regina had.

"When I'm big, I'll be a policeman!"

Kouplan hides a shudder. *Well, it'll take at least fifteen years until Liam is able to put on a police uniform and by then all of this will be solved. It will all be solved by then, right?*

How long can someone stay hidden?

He types the search into his computer, even though his brother's voice tells him to stop shrinking.

There's no good answer.

The search engine thinks he means, *how long can chlamydia stay hidden in the body?*

Someone on Flashback has wondered how you find a hidden person and is informed that the Tax Authority has a list of everyone living in Sweden. Now that's a modified truth.

The police car finally starts to roll away, slowly and steadily like a crocodile.

The prey exhales without a sound.

CHAPTER 10

When Julia was four years old, we went to the seashore. We took the bus to the stop by the swimming area and then walked past it. I walked slowly while Julia ran and jumped. She would jump over the roots of the pine trees, exposed through erosion and as thick as her arms. She stopped all at once to gape at a beetle. She leaned over it and then jumped back as it opened its coal-black wings and flew off. When I started laughing, she first imitated me and then she laughed whole-heartedly. The edge of the forest smelled like midsummer flowers.

"We haven't been to this forest," she said.

She would ask questions in the form of statements.

"It's not a real forest," I replied. "You can call it a grove. We've been here before. Once. When you were a baby."

"When I was in your tummy."

I laughed again. She laughed, too, without knowing why.

"No, after you were born. You were so little, I had to carry you everywhere."

The sunshine streamed through the branches of the pine trees and we walked a few more yards and the sun poured down. I shut my eyes to it and drew in the scent of the midsummer flowers and listened to the water, the wind, Julia's contented prattle. A bird twittered somewhere between heaven and earth, perhaps a blackbird. The bird-song landed inside me so softly and brought the world into here and now. Sun. Blackbird. Wind. How much time went by before I noticed that Julia had stopped talking. The bird started singing again and the silence hit me. I opened my eyes and could not see my child.

"Julia?"

The fight to call out softly versus scream at the top of my lungs . . . I had learned not to scream, so I hissed.

"Julia? Julia, where are you? Julia, come out, this isn't funny anymore."

I found her by the reeds. A swan was nearby, weighing about twenty pounds.

They stood, looking at each other. Julia had curious eyes and the swan was looking the way swans look. You don't play with those birds.

"Julia!"

Julia jumped back. The swan took a step toward her with its black, squelching foot.

In two seconds, I was there and swept Julia up into my arms and far away from the swan's pearl eyes. My heart was beating against Julia's back, and she probably felt it. She sniffed and I turned her toward me and smiled calmly to make her feel safe and finally she smiled, too.

"That was a really big bird," she stated. "Were you afraid it would take me away?"

I stroked her cheek and the sun continued to beam down on us.

"Yes, I was a little afraid."

"If it grabbed me," Julia said, "I would do what we practiced."

The swan was already swimming out into open water. It was beautiful from a distance. My heart had calmed down and I squatted in front of Julia.

"Show me!"

Someone not me would have thought she was having an epileptic attack.

"Let meee goooo!" she screamed and kicked into the air. She giggled and then screamed again. "I am Pernilla's child! Not this bird's! Take me to . . . where was that place?"

"Sofia Church."

"Take me to Sofia Church!"

She always forgot that her safe place was Sofia Church.

CHAPTER 11

He'd found out something else. Because the police car had
been occupying the space in front of his apartment building all morning long, he was forced to spend his time on
Internet searches.

There was something urgent he needed to figure out,
and Kouplan had to approach the issue from the right direction. He's thinking so hard about it that he forgets to
look around at the turnstiles, but all goes well anyway.
That's dangerous—it means sooner or later he'll stop being vigilant.

He decides he's going to go to the Globe Arena but
then the phone rings and it's Pernilla.

"Maybe she's at Sofia Church!" she says excitedly. "We
always agreed that we would meet there if we got sepa-
rated."

Kouplan nods, saying: "We'll meet there right away."

He's thinking deeply about this as he transfers to the

red line. He's thinking about what he's found out and what he can say to Pernilla. If the girl turns out to be at Sofia Church, he won't have to say anything at all.

Janus sees him first. The dog is ridiculously happy to see him and when Kouplan bends down to receive a few slobbering dog kisses, he feels safe. A man greeting a blond woman's excited dog—what can be less suspicious than that?

Pernilla hugs him unexpectedly. She has never hugged him before, even when he'd left her apartment. His body reacts instantly, the hug catches in his throat and he can't say a word. His body is reminding him, as naïve and open as bodies can be: *a hug feels good*. By then, she's already let go.

"We always told each other that we would meet here," she says. "I don't know if Julia remembered it. And it's locked."

She's saying this as Kouplan is studying the church doors. They are big and heavy and might be hiding a child behind them.

"Have you checked the windows?"

Most of the enormous windows of the church are high over their heads. Two are within reach if you stand on one of the backs of the benches.

"Sit on the bench!" Kouplan tells her, but she doesn't want to sit—she wants to see as much as possible: Julia safe within the warmth, being taken care of by the kind people of the church.

Still, if she were to stand with him, the bench would fall over.

So she sits down and stretches her neck in an impossible attempt to see through the window, while Kouplan is balancing on the back, holding onto the wall and lifting himself up.

"What do you see?"

"Nothing."

He tries to pull himself farther up and is standing on his toes on the back, and if he falls, she won't be able to catch him. The only thing she can do is to sit as still as possible on the bench and watch Kouplan's feet nervously. She sees that the soles of his shoes have holes.

"Nothing," he says again. He taps at the window. "It's completely dea . . . empty inside."

She hears that he almost said *dead* and his consideration for her feelings makes her want to cry. Kouplan's feet in their worn shoes jump down from the bench and he sighs and catches her eye.

"I think I'll walk around the church and see what I can see. You can stay sitting here if you want."

The words make her dizzy, the way words have ever since Julia went missing. *If I want to. What does want even mean? Especially if I only want one thing and it's not sitting on a bench?*

Kouplan doesn't leave.

"How are you holding up?" he asks, holding out his hand in a meaningless gesture.

She draws in a deep breath so that she doesn't die. Looks as far away into the heavens as she can. *What does this mean, how am I holding up?*

"Let's take a walk together around the church," she says, as she forces her body to feel lighter than lead. "But she's not here."

She's not here. Kouplan feels it because Pernilla feels it, but he takes her for a walk around the church anyway. Her nose is red and he knows it's not the chill.

"Do you often come here together?" he asks and is careful to put his question in the present tense.

"Not lately, but we were here often when Julia was younger. It was the only place where we . . ."

She falls silent and he looks at her. Like one frightened deer to another. What has she been part of?

"What . . ." he begins and then changes his question. "How did they help you here?"

Pernilla's eyes flutter and she is looking over the brick walls and up into the ice blue heavens.

"There was a priest here. I don't know if it's the same priest. He was . . . well . . . good. I'm a little sensitive."

She turns toward him as she says that last word. Her face is more open than he's seen before.

"I'm sensitive to certain things. And there are some people who just accept you for who you are."

What things? He wants to ask. *What made you so sensitive?*

Instead he asks, "What was the priest's name?"

"Thor. I don't know his last name."

Kouplan writes this name into his brain. It's easy to remember. Thor, the Norse god of war.

"Do you go to church?" asks Pernilla.

"Never."

"You're not religious?"

"Not at all."

"But you don't eat pork."

"No, I don't."

He comes with her to her apartment. It seems more important than going to the Globe Arena and meeting more questioning eyes and negative responses. There are a few things he needs to know about Pernilla and these are the kinds of questions you just can't ask in the middle of the street.

"Aren't you going to keep searching for Julia?" asks Pernilla.

She's putting her key into the lock.

"I'm doing it right now."

He can't tell her that her odd behavior is hampering his investigation. If only she wouldn't be as closed up as an oyster.

"I have three lines of inquiry," he says instead. "I need some more information from you before I can go further in the investigation."

"What kind of information?"

"Let's sit down first."

A real detective would open his laptop. Kouplan opens his light blue notebook from his class in Swedish as a Second Language.

"One line of inquiry is Patrick. But I don't think he's involved."

Pernilla shakes her head.

"No, he's not."

"I'm going to follow up, just to be sure. Make a few calls. Anyway . . . the next line of inquiry is a rumor of a guy who trades in people. I'm going to go back to the Globe Arena and check if anyone has seen him."

Pernilla is staring at him.

"What if he's the one?"

He sees the fear in her eyes and remembers the disgust in Rashid's voice when he mentioned M.B. He puts conviction and warmth into his voice.

"If he's involved, Julia is alive."

"Why would he take her?"

Kouplan puts his hand on his warm coffee cup. *Yes, why her? And why did he end up in this exact apartment, in this exact country, in this exact body, sitting across from this exact woman?*

"These things happen sometimes," he replies. "And then, I have one last line of inquiry: People who knew Julia."

"Yes, I'm trying to remember if there was anyone in particular . . ."

"I'm going to the library tomorrow morning as I think they're closed now. And I'll also follow up on Thor."

"On Thor?"

"You told me he helped you and Julia. So he must have liked her."

She nods in a way that neither confirms nor denies what he says.

"Of course, but why would he be the one who took her?"

"Maybe she came to the church as you agreed. And he took her in, especially if he didn't know where you lived? Or maybe he contacted the police?"

She stiffens, her coffee cup in her hand. A wave shimmers over the dark brown surface.

"No, he wouldn't. He'd take care of her until I would come for her. Yes, that's exactly what he would do."

She's nodding at her own words as she looks into his eyes. He can see that she has hope that Julia is safe and sound at Thor the priest's place. But Kouplan has met all too many priests to feel the same way.

"So those are the lines of inquiry," he says. "I'm going to go home and get something to eat and then I'll finish up with Patrick, just to rule him out."

"Okay."

"First, however, I need you to answer an extremely important question."

It's been the question on his mind since that morning. Ever since he'd been searching on the web to find numerous men with the initials M.B. That led him to the Tax Authority.

He puts down his coffee cup and looks right at Pernilla.

"Why isn't Julia Svensson registered with the Tax Authority?"

CHAPTER 12

Pernilla doesn't answer right away, but he lets the question hang in the air until she finally catches it. She looks at him searchingly.

"I don't know if you would understand."

Kouplan, for one of one hundred thousand reasons, in this country, in this apartment, in this body, also does not have an identification number.

"I understand most things," he says, and truthfully he does.

"Well, then," Pernilla says. "Let me pour myself another cup of coffee first."

She heads into the kitchen, a being in jeans and a cardigan, full of sorrow and secrets. A body that once carried a child who is gone. An amputated life, like his.

If she did carry the child herself. A suspicion comes to mind, and he wants to ignore it, but he must think about it now that he's a real detective: *Was Julia always her child from the beginning?*

Pernilla's hand is shaking as she sets her second cup of coffee down on the table.

"What do you know about Social Services?"

Kouplan shrugs. If it's the same bureaucracy he's had to deal with, he knows he can't get help from them without a residence permit.

"Social Services evaluates whether or not you can keep your child. If you are competent. You see?"

"And why would you not be competent?"

Pernilla shivers and pulls her feet under her body. It makes her appear like a girl, even though she's certainly over thirty.

"I had some problems when I was young. When I met Patrick, I was feeling better for a while, but I had problems again when I was pregnant. Take a look."

She pulls up her sleeves and shows her pale lower arms to Kouplan. Pure white scars show a lifetime of despair and calming razor blades.

"Patrick sent me to the psych ward and I was kept there . . . I was there a few times, and I can't even remember how many. You must think I'm crazy, now, right?"

She is staring at him worriedly. He thinks that all the scars on her arms are chalk white. None of them are new. He shakes his head.

"I don't think you're crazy."

She releases her fear and breath in one long sigh. Pulls her legs even tighter under her body.

"I knew that they wouldn't let me keep Julia."

Silence told the rest of the story. Kouplan fills it in.

"So you faked a miscarriage."

"I gave birth to Julia here in this room all by myself."

Kouplan is living in a country where the citizens have everything arranged for them. That's how he thinks about the Swedes. Like an Excel spreadsheet where the grid pattern and the calculations keep them from falling and they call it cradle-to-grave welfare. Pernilla's story is a deviation from the rules, a dizzying drop out of the system. As is Julia, the girl, who is hardly a citizen, just as he is not. He tries to take it in as Pernilla explains.

"If she doesn't exist, they can't take her away from me."

She's pulling down her sleeves and covering the white streaks with her kaftan. She's drinking the coffee, that's already getting cold, and breathes in air as if it were cocaine. Kouplan looks around the room where Julia was born. He tries to imagine a blond Swede giving birth to her child alone on a linoleum floor and, presumably, layers of towels. Pernilla turns back to him and her face is as naked as it had been outside the church.

"And now someone *has* taken her."

Kouplan can't exactly get up and leave for lunch after hearing a story like that. Although the coffee is keeping the worst hunger pangs away, it also eats into his stomach.

"I'm going to make a sandwich," Pernilla says. "Want one?"

He has four in all: cheese and green bell pepper. He wants more, but you can't eat as many sandwiches as you want in someone else's house.

"Go ahead," she says. "Take another one. Have you eaten yet today?"

He contemplates her. Karin has always told him not to tell anyone, ever. He spreads butter onto a slice of bread with Pernilla's green plastic butter knife and then he tells her:

"I don't exist, either."

Something about secrets weighs down a person's soul. A human being's secrets are walls and shrinking rooms— or waiting for seventy-five lashes of the whip. The feeling humans have when they keep secrets means they're not made for telling lies.

"I'm hiding from the border police," Kouplan says, although he knows he shouldn't.

He's afraid, but he's breathing more freely.

"I knew there was something about you," Pernilla says.

He thinks she gives him a longer hug as they say goodbye. Longer than the one she gave him when they met at the church. She smells of perfumed soap and she's warm and her cheek is soft. Her white scars are warming his neck.

Back in his room, he searches: *Social Services take children.* He needs to understand, to check it out. One mother gives tips to other mothers who have lost their children to Social Services. One discussion page has hundreds of leads on how to hide from them and one title reads: *Soc threatens to wait at the maternity ward to take my child when I give birth.* There are many of them; this is a part of Swedish society that has been hidden from him. He wonders for a while how likely it would be that someone from Social Services heard that Pernilla gave birth in secret and if they would come and take her right from the street. *Unlikely,* he concludes, but still writes up another line of inquiry. Now he has five.

CHAPTER 13

One minute on Kouplan's phone costs fifty-nine *öre*. Ten minutes is six crowns and one hour is thirty-six. The charge applies the second a new minute starts, so it's good to keep an eye on the seconds on Regina's kitchen clock.

He could call from Regina's home phone, but that could be traced.

As soon as the outer door dampens sound of yelling children and he can hear the elevator start going down, he walks into the kitchen. He takes a few deep breaths and then tests his phrases and his ultra-Swedish male voice. Then he punches in Patrick's number.

"Yes, hello," he says as soon as Patrick picks up. "My name is Robert Johansson. I have some questions about a certain Pernilla Svensson. Have I reached the right number?"

"No."

The reply is immediate.

Kouplan hums in that questioning way Swedes have.

"That's odd. Aren't you Patrick Magnusson? Former live-in partner of Pernilla?"

"Who the hell are you?"

"She gave you as a reference," Kouplan lies smoothly. "But you say you don't know her?"

"How the hell did you get my number? I don't have anything to do with that psycho, nothing whatsoever."

"You do know who she is."

"Look here!"

The way Patrick says *look here* in such an authoritative manner is something Kouplan will store in case he needs to sound authoritative himself later on.

"If you meet Pernilla, tell her to leave me the hell alone. I've moved on."

"And Julia, who is your d . . ."

"Who the hell are you?" Patrick interrupts with a voice barely under control. "You said you got me as a reference. A reference for what, if I may ask?"

Kouplan is about to say that Julia is missing and involve Patrick in the search for his daughter, but he realizes this is definitely not a good idea. Perhaps Patrick is involved or might go to the police himself.

"Pernilla said . . ."

"Hey, know what? We're done here. Tell her to stop trying to get in contact with me and you, don't you ever call me again."

Click. Second fifty-eight. Say what you will about Patrick, he saved Kouplan fifty-nine öre. *Does not like Per-*

nilla one bit, he writes next to Patrick's name in his notebook. *Doesn't give a damn about Julia. Doesn't know Julia is his child? Is she even his child?*

How could he figure out whether or not Pernilla was telling the truth about Patrick being the father when Patrick doesn't want to talk about her? It's not like they sell DNA tests at the corner store. He notes: *How many men were in Pernilla's life seven years ago?*

His second call goes to Sofia Church. A woman picks up the phone. She doesn't recognize the name: Thor.

With a laugh, she says, "I've only been here six months, though."

Her voice is warm like a blanket you'd want to curl up in.

"Just a minute and let me check with someone who's worked here longer," she says and the voice disappears.

Sixty-three seconds go by on the kitchen clock as the silence cuts though Kouplan's phone, warm from his ear. He stares at his notes, tries to see if something has escaped his attention. Like Thor, the name the woman doesn't recognize. The employee at Subway, the Greek restaurant, the kiosk, but nobody has mentioned a single strange man with a child. Like Patrick, the man who didn't want to talk.

"Yes, hello, are you there? Yes, I talked to our treasurer and there was a certain Thor who used to work here. Do you have a pen and paper?"

Kouplan just happens to have those very two things.

•   •   •

It's 10:30 and Kouplan's getting off the bus in Pernilla's neighborhood. He hesitates; maybe he should let Pernilla come with him? But something in his gut tells him not to call her.

Once his brother was supposed to go to a meeting at the newspaper. He asked Kouplan if he wanted to come with him, but his guts flipped in a way that made him decline. *Thank God*, his mother said later. *Thank Allah that I didn't lose both of my children.*

Kouplan listens to his gut and walks alone across the little central area up to the glass door with LIBRARY printed in standard official lettering. Around him, people are heading to work, kids with a free hour in their schedule are buying hot dogs, and frozen elderly men and women are coming out of the State Liquor Store with violet plastic bags in their hands. Inside the library's door, it smells like a public building and literature. A brown-haired librarian is moving books from a shelf to a rolling cart. She looks at Kouplan as if she's heard wrong.

"You need the children's department?"

"Yes, where is it?"

"Over there past that bookshelf."

He feels her eyes on his back as he turns to the right past the bookshelf. It wouldn't seem so strange if he'd had a child? Or perhaps knew some?

There are red chairs and wooden tables in the children's department and a three-foot-high figure of *Emil of Lönne-*

berga. Two dads with beards and their associated kids. Babies in carriages, twin girls around five and a three-year-old boy. The children's librarian has short hair and glasses. Twenty-five at most. She smiles at Kouplan. She's slightly plump and rather cute.

"There's a woman who usually comes here with her kid," Kouplan says and shows her a picture of Pernilla on his phone.

His phone is old, so the girl has to lean forward to get a good look. He can see the top of her breasts, but doesn't have time to think about that.

"Do you recognize her?"

The shorthaired girl nods in concentration.

"Yeah, I believe I do."

"And she also has a daughter she brings here?"

"Okay. So?"

"I found this," Kouplan says and holds up his notebook. "I think it's hers. It has meetings and telephone numbers and I think it's important. But there's no name on it. Do you know anything about them?"

He can tell the girl wants to be helpful. She asks to look at the picture again. Kouplan wants to hear more about Julia.

"Her daughter is six and kind of quiet. Is there anyone here who usually talks to them?"

She takes his hand—softly puts her fingers around the back of his hand—as she turns the phone closer toward her view.

"I think I know who you're talking about. But I've

never talked to them about anything more than the rules for checking out books and that kind of thing. She's weird, right?"

She looks up toward him while still holding her fingers around his hand. For some reason, this bothers him.

"We're all a bit weird, aren't we?" he says and smiles his most charming smile to take the sting out of the fact he'd just defended Pernilla.

A real detective wouldn't have said this. A real detective would have said: *Tell me more.*

After he leaves the library and has a kebab for lunch, he takes the bus back to the Globe Arena. Not because it's been helpful before. This time, as he exits the bus, he meets two large policemen, and his first instinct is to rush down into the subway. But they're not looking at him. They're keeping an eye open for signs of sports affiliation: yellow and black or red, yellow, and blue; scarves, beer swilling, and testosterone. About ten twenty-year-olds, wearing yellow and black, strutting with gym-trained legs and exercising their bass voices, joking around too loudly as clouds of testosterone waft past him. Kouplan slinks by thankfully.

First he goes to Subway. It's filled with yellow and black scarves and there's someone else at the cashier's spot than the girl he's met before. At the Greek restaurant, it's absolutely packed. They're selling "hockey beer" for fifteen crowns and the waitress doesn't even look at him when he asks her if he can ask a few questions. Outside, riot police are milling around while scruffy men with hand-written signs wander past: *Tickets?* They don't look like they want to go to the match.

Line of Inquiry 1: Someone who needs a child. Who goes to the Globe Arena to kidnap a child? Someone disreputable, someone who already knows the arena area well. Kouplan takes a few deep breaths and ignores the police, even though they are supposedly here to protect decent citizens like himself, and walks right up to one of the men with a sign declaring: *Need tickets?*

"Tickets?" the man greets him.

Kouplan shakes his head.

"Just wondering about something."

"I'm working here."

"A single question."

They've talked for perhaps ten seconds and another ticket man is walking toward them. Kouplan realizes immediately that these ticket men are organized. Perhaps he shouldn't ask, but he does anyway.

"You guys working together?"

"There a problem here?" the new ticket man says. "They go for six hundred."

"Looking for someone," Kouplan says quickly. "Rough dude, often here. Goes by M.B."

The men look at each other.

"So you don't want to buy a ticket," the one says.

"Wait, what's the deal with this M.D.?" asks the other.

"M.B.," Kouplan repeats.

"He sell tickets?"

"All I know is he has a big nose and goes by M.B. and he hangs around here."

The larger of the two studies him, pouting.

"You don't know much, I see."

He can hear what they're doing. They're playing with him, amused by him, tickled by the mystery of a young, middle-class Iranian looking for a criminal with a big nose. They're guessing it must be about drugs. Or money.

"Here last Monday. With a girl, six years old," Kouplan says.

The two men talk to each other in their own language.

"So you don't want to buy tickets," the older one says again.

"Was he tall?" asked the younger one. "I saw a big guy here last week. I was at Mickey D's."

He nods toward McDonald's.

"He had the girl with him?"

"Yeah, that's what I'm saying."

The older man turns to his colleague.

"What were you doing here on a Monday?" he asks and the younger one opens his arms.

Behind them, two policemen are walking up.

"Was she wearing a pink raincoat?" Kouplan asks quickly and the young man wrinkles his forehead.

"Yeah, she could've been."

Kouplan keeps his heart in check as the two policemen keep coming closer, since one of them had seen Julia.

"So he had a big nose?"

The older man draws back and disappears in the

crowd, waving his sign. The policemen sweep past them toward three tipsy men in colorful scarves. Kouplan thinks about lions and zebras. Full lions don't seek prey.

"Not so big," the younger ticket seller says. "Not so big he'd be tripping over it. I remember it wasn't small, though. And that the little girl was crying . . . I think . . . and he was carrying her."

"Which way?"

The older man yells something that Kouplan doesn't understand. An order. The younger looks around, holds up the sign. Time for Kouplan to let the ticket sellers sell their tickets. Still, as he's lifting his sign, the younger one points.

"That way. Toward Skärmarbrink."

CHAPTER 14

In its way, it's a fairly normal room. It has a dresser, two chairs, and a small table. A bed. The first strange thing is that it's not hers. The man who calls himself her "real father" tells her it's her room, but it isn't. Her real room has stuffed animals and Legos. She will never call it her room. She will never call him her real dad.

The second strange thing is that the door is locked. She'd never known a locked room before, except a bathroom. If the room with the chairs and table hadn't been locked, she'd open it the minute the man went to the bathroom. She'd run all the way home to her mother. When she closes her eyes, she can sense the direction she'd run. She can tell her legs would carry her through a hundred uphill runs, and she knows very well that the room is locked to prevent her running.

●　　●　　●

She is fairly sure he's not her real dad. Maybe she'd thought so at first, because he looked her directly in the eyes as he spoke, and he was a grown-up. Is there anything more truthful, for a moment, than when a grown-up looks you in the eye as he speaks?

She feels stupid for going with him. Now, afterward, she feels so incredibly stupid, so stupid that she almost deserves to be locked up in this room. His voice and his outstretched hand deceived her into not screaming. She still hasn't screamed.

When she's about to fall asleep, she thinks of her real room. She thinks of her teddy bears and her mother's goodnight hugs. She tells herself she can't forget them.

CHAPTER 15

Kouplan leaves the Globe Arena as fast as he can. His legs hurry, but his mind puts on the brakes. Behind him, there are twenty enormous police officers.

He imagines he's M.B. and he's carrying a little girl. Over the bridge, up between the houses on Skärmarbrink. She's crying, she's frightened. If he's prepared, he would have put her to sleep with something. If he's acting on impulse, he's covering her mouth.

There are many large-nosed men in the world. He underlines this fact in his mind, so he's not blind to reality. A large-nosed man does not necessarily have to be the human trafficker that Rashid's roommates know. There could be two large-nosed men who carry small girls through the streets of Stockholm.

When he arrives at the subway, if he's still M.B. with a crying girl on his shoulder, he'll have to dig out a ticket in order to get through the turnstile. That would mean he'd have to put down the child and the child could run away. Unless he asks the ticket agent to let him through.

The man in the booth has pig eyes and psoriasis. He blinks at Kouplan.

"The day before yesterday?"

"No, Monday last week. Were you working then?"

"Ummm . . . nah . . . no, no I wasn't."

"Who was?"

The man blinks again.

"I know, but I can't tell you."

"You can't?"

"No, I'm not allowed."

For a few seconds, they look at each other, the agent and Kouplan. In silence, at a dead end.

"Well, do you think you could give him a call?"

"Maybe I could."

Kouplan tells a roundabout story about a guy with a child who dropped a backpack, which Kouplan hadn't brought back with him at the moment for a number of reasons, and the man with the pig eyes could ask why he didn't bring the backpack to lost-and-found, but he doesn't. Instead, he heaves a large sigh and pushes a Post-it note through the opening.

"Write down your number and we'll see if she wants to speak with you."

Swedish is Kouplan's fourth language. He'd learned most of it himself, by watching Swedish films ten times in a row and reading books a hundred times over. He'd probably never think of Swedish as his native language, but he knew enough that *we'll see* usually means *no*. The man would probably not call the other ticket agent; she'll probably never call him back; but Kouplan writes his number down anyway. He'll spread his questioning around Globen, Gullmarsplan, and Skärmarbrink and be like a sea turtle mother: hope that at least one survives.

Twenty minutes later, his phone rings. Unknown number. It can be the ticket agent, the man at the kiosk, the girl at the Subway. But it's Rashid.

He says he's been thinking about Kouplan.

"I was so surprised when I saw you at the grill," he says. "I couldn't bring myself to ask."

Kouplan knows what Rashid wants to ask, but has no desire to talk about it.

"Why? There's nothing to ask about," he says shortly.

"No, no . . . obviously . . . but I . . . I just wanted to know how you're doing?"

Rashid, always considerate.

"I'm fine," Kouplan said. "I got a little money from a job. Nothing criminal," he added quickly, imagining Rashid's expression of relief. "How are you doing? How's the family?"

Kouplan almost bites his tongue. He doesn't really care to know about Rashid's family.

"Bad," Rashid says. "Things are bad."

"I'm sorry."

He hears Rashid swallow a sigh, wonders where he is and whose phone he's borrowing.

"Why are you looking for . . . ?" Rashid asks a moment later. "Does it have to do with the money?"

Kouplan appreciates Rashid's censorship.

"Yes, it does," he replies. "It has to do with the actual thing I'm looking for."

"I understand," Rashid says. "You don't want to think about it. You don't want to think about others, but when you do . . ."

"Right."

"I asked around a little more and they asked why I was asking. Soon they'll be thinking I'm the one interested in little girls."

Rashid seemed to have lifted his self-censorship. Kouplan waits for Rashid to continue.

"Nobody knows where she is. Nobody knows where *he* is. But there's this interesting thing . . . the gossip starts to circulate . . . so my questions have gone out and some answers have come back. There's a schoolgirl, about seven years old. Blond. It turns my stomach, but . . . Kouplan, it's like they're advertising her."

It would turn Kouplan's stomach, too, if he let this information reach his heart.

"She could be six years old. If they're saying she's around seven, she could be six," Kouplan said, mostly to himself.

"You have to be very careful," Rashid said. "This is no boy scout we're dealing with. And we have nobody to turn to, remember."

"I understand. Thanks, Rashid."

Kouplan would have never met Rashid if the two of them hadn't had their asylum rejected. In other circumstances, they could laugh and joke on their own phones with legitimate accounts, they could hang out together, and Rashid's wife and kids wouldn't have anything more to worry about than the October darkness.

"There's hope in hopelessness," Kouplan says. "The day always follows the night."

All he has is a proverb. It seems empty, says as much about hopelessness as about hope.

Rashid answers like all the guys at the grill.

"*Insha'Allah.*"

The police are never on the bus. Like, almost never. That's why Kouplan is feeling at ease as he rides to Pernilla's. That's why he's taking the bus over there instead of calling. The trees and the roads around her house seem like places the police never go.

There are things he's been thinking about ever since he met Pernilla. Something about her reaction to the loss of her child. He knows the stages people go through in crisis: shock, denial, prayer, fear, rage, despair, acceptance. Not just because he's read about them, but also because he's seen them. He thinks that Pernilla must still be in shock. But perhaps also in denial, perhaps also afraid. But also something he can't put his finger on. Today she's been washing the windows.

"I have to think about something else," she says. "It's easier if I keep busy so I don't think about it."

Kouplan knows. His own mother baked cookies frenetically after his brother disappeared. *All the craziness has to leave through the hands*, she'd said, *rather than seep into the brain*. They ate cookies for weeks. He can still taste the sweetly sour flavor of his brother's absence. So he ought to recognize desperation.

"How good you can get it out in a positive way," he said, looking at the rubber squeegee still in her hand.

Pernilla hears his undertone.

"So that I don't slit my wrists, you mean."

Kouplan starts to blush, but doesn't follow up on his embarrassment.

"Pernilla, about Julia," he starts to say instead. "Is she tall for her age? I mean, could people mistake her for a seven-year-old?"

Something in Pernilla's eyes shifts. Kouplan wishes he didn't have to ask about Julia; that Pernilla could simply continue to clean windows therapeutically a little longer. Her upper lip curls, reminding Kouplan of a child who's lost her teddy bear.

"Yes," she replies with a sharp intake of breath. "Yes, maybe she could be taken for being older. Not a nine or ten-year-old, that's for sure, but maybe a seven-year-old. Why are you asking?"

"I don't have a photo of Julia," Kouplan answers. "So if someone says they've seen a seven-year-old girl . . ."

"Has someone seen her?"

Her eyes become crazy, wild, concerned. She has the right to hear about M.B.

"No," he says, and her eyes calm down.

Theoretically, it's not a lie. Neither Rashid nor his roommates have seen the girl.

"So Julia is blond and looks like you," he says. "Can you tell me any more details about her looks?"

Pernilla sighs deeply: takes in a lung-full of air and lets it out.

"Are you hungry?"

The sun goes down three minutes earlier every evening. It's already dark when Kouplan gets on the bus, eight meat-balls warming his stomach, and he thinks that those three missing minutes are noticed most in October. They come with the cold that goes through jeans, scarves, earflaps— frozen people can't afford to look from side to side— another way to protect the self.

He's written down everything Pernilla told him in his notebook. Pernilla couldn't remember things well at first, but after he asked her many questions, he finally had a good description. *Blond hair, narrow face, thin. About 128 centimeters tall, no birth marks. Thin but normal lips. (Thinner than Pernilla's.)*

On the lines above it, he's written down the details about the man he plans to meet tomorrow. He hasn't told Pernilla about it.

These three minutes of extra darkness—he really doesn't need them. He can feel them dig deep into his soul, pull him back into the nothingness he's lived in for much too long. Pernilla had to clean the windows in order not to go crazy thinking about Julia. Kouplan had to search for Julia so the darkness wouldn't eat at his soul.

The meatballs had been made of chicken. She'd smiled as she told him, even showing him the list of ingredients on the box.

"The ones I usually buy have pork," she'd said as she emptied the carton into the frying pan. As if it were completely normal to change your meatball brand in order to match your private detective's eating preferences. As he thinks about it, he realizes that Pernilla has made sure he's had something to eat each time he'd been by. Each and every time.

What if someone offers him pork tomorrow?

The thought hits him as he gets off the blue line and walks quickly to Regina's apartment. If he's offered a hot dog, should he say no? He has no idea what Swedish priests think about Muslims. There's always the risk they're no different from everyone else.

When he puts his key in the lock, he realizes he's solved this problem. If Thor, the priest, offers him hot dogs, he'll just do the most Swedish thing of all: say he's allergic.

CHAPTER 16

Thor lives in a wooden house surrounded by a fence and wrought-iron gate. Between the house and the fence are several meters of lawn and bushes. Kouplan finds himself searching for the kind of bomb shelter a Swedish gardening expert would have situated behind the house—if Sweden had been at war. Instead, roses are growing, beautiful in so many ways. He strides to the front door. There's some kind of metal doorknocker with a name on it. Two more quick steps and he gives it a knock.

Something about men in religious life leads to beards. Christianity says nothing about facial hair, so probably this has to do with Swedish priest culture picturing bearded prophets and old men on clouds. Thor follows this convention. His well-groomed goatee declares: "Hi, I'm a deep-thinking and pleasant guy who knows how to use a trimmer." In other countries, a mustache would have made the same declaration.

"Welcome," Thor says. "Come on in."

Just like men with mustaches, he doesn't reveal if he is bewildered by Kouplan's visit. Or nervous. He gestures to where Kouplan can hang his jacket, walks him past two paintings depicting moose into the living room with its brown leather furniture.

"I'd like to know why you think you need my help," he says, while he pours tea for them without asking first. "You'd been speaking with someone from Sofia?"

Kouplan nods, takes a sip of the boiling hot tea, nods again.

"I'm looking for someone who knows Pernilla Svensson," he says.

Thor slurps loudly and meets Kouplan's eyes with his own steel-gray ones.

"Unfortunately, I can't tell you whether I've met her or not. Professional confidentiality."

"But I met her. She, herself, told me she'd met you."

"Then I don't understand. If you've met with her, why do you need to talk to me?"

Kouplan shakes his head as he picks up the cookie the priest has offered.

"I need to talk to you because she mystifies me. She said you were the only person who ever accepted her as she is."

Thor sighs deeply, picks up a cookie, and puts the whole thing in his mouth. This keeps him from speaking for a moment. His goatee bobs up and down as his jaws chew frenetically.

"I cannot reveal whom I have met as part of my work.

That's in my contract. But there're some general insights I can share."

Kouplan pricks up his ears and tries not to appear impatient.

"In general," Thor repeats with emphasis, "I can say that, in conversation, I do my best to make a person feel understood, even when it is difficult to be understood. Or believed. But there are different schools of thought as far as this is concerned. Lots of discussion. How does one help someone who is lost?"

His gray eyes bore into Kouplan's as if demanding an answer to his question, which, in all honesty, is fairly nebulous.

"By trying to force her to go where she doesn't want to go? Or by taking her hand and asking her where her soul strives to go?"

Kouplan catches his breath as he realizes the meaning behind the priest's questions. Which answer would have been the one the most helpful to him? A thought begins to bubble up in his mind, but he represses it. His body has given him the answer.

"So you took Pernilla's hand," he says.

He should not have mentioned Pernilla by name. The direct statement reminds the priest of his professional confidentiality and he smiles that pious smile that is probably taught in divinity school.

"Perhaps you might want to tell me why you decided to look me up. Your questions regarding Pernilla. Do they also apply to you? Are you seeking something yourself?"

Kouplan understands why Pernilla put her trust in this priest. He can almost hear Pernilla and the priest talking to each other. Thor's considerate, deeply personal questions. But Kouplan does not need psychotherapy. At least, that's not why he is here.

"It's Julia, her daughter," he says. "She's disappeared."

He's certain that the priest reacts to the mention of Julia's name. The man's jaws clench a fleeting moment; he draws in one breath. After that, nothing more to indicate anything.

"I am sorry," Thor says. "I cannot tell you anything regarding a specific person."

This is a strange reaction for someone who has just heard that a child is missing. A normal person would exclaim: *Oh my God, she's gone missing?* The face would blanch. Exclamations. Questions about calling the police. But this priest has an uncanny control over his reactions when they fall under professional confidentiality. There is real compassion in his gaze, but again, several times, he replies he can say no more.

One, two, three, Kouplan's brain sorts his thoughts into alternatives. Number one: Swedes don't react when children go missing. Number two: Thor knows something about Pernilla that makes him not surprised by this information. Number three: Thor knows what has happened.

He has the feeling that his investigative methods have been completely ineffectual up to now. He's taken a peek into Patrick's home and seen a statue and a flower vase.

Observed the décolletage of a librarian. He has to be, he *is*, smarter than that.

"I've never been in a priest's home before," he says using his most charming smile.

Thor chuckles at this revelation.

"I hope my humble abode isn't a disappointment."

Whatever abode means, it doesn't seem to make the goateed priest nervous. Or he hides it well.

"I've never even been in a house this large in Sweden," Kouplan adds. "We only lived in apartments."

Thor snaps at the bait. Or realizes it would seem odd not to.

Line one. Line two.

"Would you like a tour, then?"

Kouplan and the priest view a kitchen with pinewood tables and chairs, a bedroom with even more moose paintings on the walls, a bathroom with butterflies on the shower curtain, a spiral staircase to the second floor. As they walk, Thor asks where Kouplan comes from. He says he's from Afghanistan. Just in case someone comes to Thor and asks. Or if Thor goes to someone and asks. Kouplan cannot trust the priest with his pious smile and steel-gray eyes, not for a second.

"This door leads to the pantry," Thor says. "This one to the basement."

Kouplan studies the doors and tries one of them, mostly to see the priest's reaction, but his glance reveals nothing more than jam jars and sacks of potatoes. The other door is locked.

"We usually keep that door locked," Thor says. "Over here is the guest bathroom. And on the second floor, we just have our children's former bedrooms."

He takes Kouplan's hands between his when they say goodbye. He doesn't shake them, but holds them, like a priest.

"Good luck," he says. "Pernilla is lucky to have you on her side."

After a long pause, he says, "Help her."

"Help her?" Spinning threads of thought from their hour-long conversation twist through Kouplan's mind as he heads off down the gravel path and through the wrought-iron gate. He thinks about each one, stops at any that seem odd; tries to see what it means to trust Thor versus not to trust him. *"How do you turn yourself into not being a suspect?"* he thinks as he walks past Thor's neighbors, turns right, and turns right again. *"You tell the detective to help the victim, you take his hands in yours and offer a tour of the house. You blame professional confidentiality,"* Kouplan thinks as he wriggles his thin body back through rose bushes and a loose board.

The house is lit, not upstairs where the children's bedrooms are, but on the ground floor. This means the darkness is darker for those peering out than for those outside. Kouplan creeps among the rose bushes, tries not to think about floodlights and alarm systems and calms himself by thinking that Thor hasn't put in a security door.

When he's crawled to the basement window, his body is full of adrenaline. His knock at the pane seems to be so loud to him that he's sure the sound could reach any priest at all, but Kouplan keeps his eyes on the darkness on the other side of the dirty glass. If a girl's white face looks back at him, if she starts to scream, what will he do?

No girl's face looks up at him. He's a guy in dirty jeans in another man's garden, a misplaced guy lying glued to the ground and staring at paint cans and broken chairs, and then he sees them. He wriggles backward, more embarrassed than frightened now. Once he's back on the sidewalk, he brushes the dirt off his clothes as best he can.

When he's on the bus, the bus driver stares at him and adrenaline shoots through him again. *What's he looking at?* Are there immigration police on the buses these days? Is the bus driver a policeman in disguise? Only when half the ride is over does he discover that he has two dry, brown leaves in his hair.

It's been evening for a long time when the phone rings. Kouplan has eaten couscous with chicken nuggets, ten crowns a bag at Willy's. He's Googled *M.B.* and kept scanning *buying sex, prostitutes, children, women, cheap.* He thinks, *That disgusting excuse for a human being is out there somewhere.* He thinks about Pernilla, about Thor, about what they're not saying, what kind of food he could be making if he didn't have to share the fridge with Regina and the children. And that's when the phone rings, and it's someone named Melinda.

"Kalle said you'd been looking for me," she says.

Kouplan is silent, racking his brain trying to remember when he'd been looking for someone named Melinda or been talking to someone named Kalle.

"I work at the subway booth. Hello?"

Melinda. The name sounds like angel chimes to his ears. *Thank you Melinda, for giving me those extra seconds to think. Thank you for taking Kalle's wrinkled note with my number on it and calling me. Thank you that you remember when a large man carried a small girl through the gate over a week ago.*

And especially thank you for remembering where he was going.

CHAPTER 17

The large man, probably with a large nose, who carried a girl was supposed to go to Hökarängen. If he wasn't that guy, then it was the one carrying a cello, but one of the two was going to Hökarängen and Melinda was pretty sure it was the man with the girl. The girl was crying and the father seemed to have a hard time calming her down, paying for his ticket, and getting the two of them through the barrier at the same time. *Like he wasn't used to it*, Kouplan thinks, as he inspects Hökarängen's subway station.

Hundreds of Hökarängen residents are going to work, and Kouplan puts on a sufficiently harried expression to blend in. On the platform, there are at least five men who have enough volume to be considered large. All of them are alone.

As he exits the station, he thinks he wouldn't take the subway if he had a little girl he didn't know. He'd make sure he had a car in the vicinity. On the other hand, Kouplan doesn't have a car and maybe M.B. doesn't have one either, even if he pulls in a great deal of money as a swine in the sex trade.

However, if he got Julia to come with him of her own volition, it wouldn't be so strange to take the subway. Though why would she follow this man of her own volition?

Next to the subway station, there's a newsstand and a mailbox.

The newsstand guy glares at him with a look Kouplan is starting to get used to. The look that says, *What kind of an idiot are you anyway?*

"Nah . . ." he says. "Or, like, I know hundreds of people who come through here with kids every day. Then I forget them when the next customer comes in."

"But maybe you'll remember this guy. He probably looks a little shady, a little fishy. Big guy, big nose . . . usually doesn't have kids with him. But that day he did."

The newsstand guy gives him that look again, now mixed with mistrust.

"Why do you want to find him?"

"Do you know who he is?"

"No clue."

At the local grocery, there's not a lot of space between the rows of shelves, even though not many people are shopping there in the morning. A sign announces that they've expanded, so it's easy to imagine how crowded it was before. A kid around high school age is stocking the shelves with cans of crushed tomatoes.

"So, shady like a wino?"

"Well, more like a gangster, mafia-type."

"Has tattoos?"

"No," Kouplan says without knowing whether M.B. has tattoos or not. "Just the kind of big guy you'd be a little scared of, like, you wouldn't want to hang out with him."

"Kind of a fat guy?"

"Don't know. Just that he's a big guy."

The young man looks at him skeptically.

"Maybe you should start by knowing who you're looking for."

The kid has a point, but Kouplan decides he'll talk to the girl at the cash register anyway.

"Seriously, everybody has kids here," she tells him. "Absolutely everybody."

"But this is a man who didn't have a kid before and suddenly has one."

"Okay," the girl says. "Okay, no, I don't know. But if I see someone like that, I can tell him you're looking for him."

Kouplan feels the chill of ice. Only after he gets the two at the grocery store to promise, on their honor, to never say a word to the big, but not necessarily fat, man who probably does not have a tattoo but definitely has a large nose, does he feel he can breathe again and continue his questioning at Hökarängen's center. At the pharmacy, nobody has sold a suspicious amount of children's medicine to shady guys with frightened daughters approximately six years old. At the clothing store, nobody has sold children's jackets. In the hardware store, the owner has extensive knowledge on the qualities of sixteen different light bulbs, but nobody has noticed anyone who has bought things in order to build, for instance, a secret basement room. There's not a trace of the man who went to Hökarängen in Hökarängen itself.

In the cold outside, on a bench by the subway, two grizzled men are holding cans of extra strong beer. When Kouplan asks, they rattle off the names of big men: Lasse, Tompa, Kjelle, and Berra, adding, "But he's great, a really nice guy."

"Is it something you bought?" one of them asks curiously.

Kouplan doesn't get it at first.

"Bought?"

"Or were you selling? Someone stiffed you?"

He gets it now and shakes his head.

The other alcoholic glares at him.

"You Kurdish?"

"No."

"My sister married a Kurd."

"I see."

"He thinks he's so special. He should be grateful we took him in. Our taxes pay for guys like you, have you thought about that? Now I'm not allowed to see my own nieces and nephews!"

Kouplan doesn't ask how much in taxes the men in front of him have paid compared to the amount of money they're now consuming from the state. Detectives and

journalists don't rile up people unless they absolutely
have to. He gives them his number in case they hear anything. Then he leaves Hökarängen.

Detectives and journalists know you have to dig hard
where it's most uncomfortable. And the most uncomfortable thing he can think of right now is interrogating Pernilla some more. Really interrogate her. He even writes
down his questions according to importance. Then he
doesn't get to ask them, because Pernilla is crying.

"She's dead," she says between sobs as she lets him
into her apartment.

Pernilla's cheeks are shining red and damp and at first
Kouplan believes that Julia's body has been found. But
how would Pernilla know that, if she hadn't been . . .
Kouplan gives her a hug and she sinks into him, her
soft body against his thin one, her snot dripping on his
neck.

"She's dead," Pernilla says again. "I can feel it."

Mothers can feel those things. He knows this, he believes this, or he hopes this. His own mother had long felt
that his brother was alive. Pernilla keeps sobbing, more
strongly than ever, and then she's hyperventilating. So he
leads her to the sofa and has her sit down. If he knew her
better, he would have slapped her, but in this country you
can be reported for that.

So he says, "Hey. Hey, Pernilla. *Hey.*"

She stiffens as if she's seeing him for the first time.

"Breathe!" he commands. "In, out, yes, like that. Look at me. Why do you think this?"

Pernilla starts to relax and soon she's caught her breath and breathes more easily. "I feel it," she says. "Two weeks have gone by. It's Friday and we usually watch *Gladiators* together. And that . . . two weeks are . . . that two weeks . . ."

Kouplan swallows. He's already realized two weeks have gone by. When he'd sat her on the sofa, he'd released her hug, and it would be imprudent to give her another one. Instead, he pats her shoulder and feels how paltry his comfort is compared to everything.

"Nobody has found a child," he says. "If they had, it would be on the news."

Pernilla is silent.

"You've been brooding too much over possibilities," he continues. He doesn't know if he should give her hope.

But how can you not give hope to another human being?

"Are you just worried?" he asks. "Or do you actually feel deep down that she's truly dead?"

Pernilla shivers and Kouplan can feel the trembling beneath his hand.

"No," she says after some hesitation. "At first, I didn't feel that she was dead, exactly. The word *dead* didn't come into my mind. Something was just telling me that I had to let her go."

Kouplan studies her—that soft woman sitting against

her mocha sofa cushions. He can't ask questions one and two, not while tears are still trembling on her eyelashes. But the third question is one he can ask, one he ought to ask.

"When you were a child, did anything bad happen to you?"

She doesn't answer at first. Just looks at the walls and the TV, which isn't on, as if they could help her find the words. He waits. Finally, she nods and looks at him.

"Yeah, something did."

Pernilla says nothing about what happened when she was young, but it's almost as if she had. Her manner changes, is less heavy, as if with one question Kouplan had touched the heart of the matter. She feels her expression is as open as a newborn.

"I'm not a psychologist," Kouplan says. "But my mother is."

It's the first time Kouplan has mentioned his family. Did she begin to think he didn't have one? A crazy idea, of course.

"She says that if you give up, it's as if you believe you deserve nothing better. And if you believe that, it's because something happened to you earlier in your life."

She looks at him and he looks back, meeting her gaze. He has long, curved eyelashes, almost feminine. No blond Swede has eyelashes like that. No one has ever looked into her eyes like this for so long.

"So I could feel I don't deserve Julia?" she says, her words burning in her throat. "My own daughter?"

"I'm not a psychologist," Kouplan replies.

Pernilla stares at him and inwardly feels rage; not a single fiber of her being is ready to let Julia go.

"Obviously not," she says.

"I'm sorry."

Saying sorry means admitting you're wrong; he loses and she wins. She remains in that triumphant feeling for a moment, staring at the young man sitting on her sofa instead of looking for her daughter.

"You're not much of a detective, either."

She feels the unkind words echo in her mind. He looks at her for a long time. What is he thinking behind those dark eyes? Is he angry? Probably. But his expression does not change.

"Still, I have some questions that will help me become a better detective," he says.

He pulls out his childish notebook from his bag.

"First question," he says. "What was going on during the year before you had Julia?"

In his notebook, he has not written the question in those words. Instead it reads:

پدر این کودک کیست؟

"Who is the child's father?" But even Kouplan knows you have to ask that kind of question with finesse. He makes his voice as kind as possible.

"I need to know who you were meeting. Those who were friends and those who weren't."

"Why do you need to know that?"

"It's needed for background. You told me you weren't feeling well when you were pregnant. How did you feel before then?"

Her reaction is immediate. Her entire face closes off, her entire body. Wrong question. Or, perhaps, the question was exactly right.

"I thought you were going to look for Julia, not terrorize me in my own living room."

She leaps up from the sofa, knocking over her water glass. There's a Swedish expression: *Stepping on sore toes*. It fits this moment. The point is not to keep stepping on a painful spot, but he follows Pernilla into the kitchen anyway.

"I *am* trying to find Julia, do you hear me? But you need to answer my questions! I'm not going to report you! Look at me!"

He keeps saying this until she does.

"Look at me, I'm a nobody."

His own words hurt him, because they are true. Even though he almost feels like a somebody at Pernilla's house.

She leans against the fridge with a grimace.

"I felt fine. I wasn't in the psych ward, if that's what you're asking."

"I'm not making a judgment one way or the other. Did you go to church?"

"Julia and me?"

"No, you and Patrick, before Julia came. Did you attend Sofia Church?"

She shakes her head so slightly it's hard to notice.

"Not Patrick."

That's what he'd suspected. You should always keep your mind open.

"Did you go other places on your own? Did you meet someone else, I mean, someone other than Patrick?"

Pernilla is about to say something, but she interrupts herself and glares at Kouplan.

"You mean, did I *sleep* with someone else? Right? Is that what you're implying?"

He sighs and can hear Patrick's words: *that psycho*. Thinks Pernilla would start arguing. So he makes his voice as gentle as possible. Hopefully calming.

"I'm just trying to get to the truth."

Pernilla leans her head against the door. He can feel her exhaustion across two meters of air. She takes a few deep breaths, then pushes it all away with a gesture of her hands, and gives herself enough energy to take the three steps to the pantry.

"I'm so worn out," she says. "Do you drink wine?"

The gladiators wear war paint and are oiled up. The moderator introduces them: They have names like Wolf, Hero, Bullet. Kouplan lets two mouthfuls of wine run down his gullet. He'd also chosen his own name a while back. Perhaps he should have chosen a much tougher name: Zap, Fire, or something Swedish like Håg. Does Håg sound cool in Swedish? He's not the right person to know.

"Could a gladiator have a name like Håg?" he asks

Pernilla. Her glance back at him is amused, the first pleased look of the evening.

"Håg?"

"Yes, Håg."

He swallows another mouthful, then tenses up like a gladiator and says in his deepest voice:

"HÅÅÅÅG."

Pernilla almost giggles aloud. He can imagine what her giggle would sound like. She's had her first glass and has moved on to her second. She pours from a bottle, not a box.

"I have no idea what the word *håg* even means," she says. "Just that it's used in old expressions."

Pernilla reflects on Kouplan's questions. She wishes she could answer them better, but something is blocked. Like when someone is kind, but also not kind. Like forgetting the bad things so you can see them clearly. It's blocked like that: Her whole body tells her she doesn't want to know. On the television, Toro tosses a rose to the crowd.

Kouplan thinks about everything Pernilla has told him about Julia, as the wine opens up new tracks in his mind. Like Julia not being registered—what if she really is? What if he's really looking for a child who belongs to someone else? Because there's truth and then again there is truth behind the lie. If this is the case, then Pernilla might have kidnapped Julia as a baby, because he's seen the bibs and pacifiers. Or perhaps she didn't register Julia because she didn't want the real father to know about the birth. He catches his breath and scratches down this thought in his notebook before he looks again at the television program. A rather lightly clad Lynx is wrestling with her somewhat tawnier opponent on a hanging platform.

"It's amazing how they keep their clothes on," Pernilla says.

CHAPTER 18

There is one large and one enormous Dala horse at the center of Skansen. When we went to Skansen, Julia and I, she was not impressed by the bears or the moose, but always wanted to go to the Dala horses. We'd go there starting in March. I'd bring cheese sandwiches and we'd climb onto their broad wooden backs. They gave us a sense of security with the log cabins around us and then the whole fence surrounding all of Skansen itself. We were sitting on the enormous horse with Julia and me carrying on a conversation.

"There's a daddy," Julia said.

We looked at the daddy walking past pushing a baby carriage.

"Yes, there's one," I said. "Look over there—there's another one."

From our positions on the enormous horse, we watched daddies go past.

"I don't have a daddy," Julia said.

I remember the taste of cheese and bread crumbling in my saliva. With one hand, I held onto Julia and with the other I unscrewed the top of the Thermos.

"Do you want some hot chocolate?"

We shared the cup from the Thermos between us. I can still hear her voice as I'd asked her what she wanted to eat.

"Same as you."

I believe it gave her the same sense of security as the small farmyards around us.

"Do you want a daddy?"

Julia watched another one walk by and then she looked at me. "No, they're too much trouble."

She was barely three years old, but she knew how to express herself.

She was also more correct than she realized.

"It's better the way it is now," I agreed.

I didn't tell her about Patrick until several years later. I told her that he could have been her father, but he didn't want to take the chance.

That was last year.

Julia never wanted to go to the petting zoo. That was good, because I didn't like going there myself.

"Too many people," I told her. "And we don't want to run into difficult people."

She agreed with me. Especially when there were special activities, we kept our distance. We could live without the tiny theater, and the crowds of school groups scared her. But that day, when we'd been talking about daddies, we walked on the path through the petting zoo. Next to the goats, she spied a squirrel. I stopped as she walked closer. If I'd moved an inch, the squirrel would have run up a tree, but it wasn't bothered by Julia. As she reached out a hand to pet the squirrel, I became nervous. It could have rabies or God knows what, I thought, and I must have moved slightly, because the squirrel jumped, ran over the gravel path and straight up a spruce. Julia looked at me reproachfully.

"You mean I can't even play with a squirrel?"

She had a special way of expressing herself, ever since she learned to talk. She was a special child. She *is* a special child.

I wonder if that is why they took her. Did they see how special she was by her eyes? I don't know if I should hope that's why or not, but something in me hopes that's why.

You can go to Skansen for free if you are a child under six. Next summer, she'd need a ticket.

CHAPTER 19

He's in police custody. He can smell dust and cleaning fluid, as well as coffee from their coffee machine, and he doesn't dare open his eyes. The coffee machine sputters and steams; do they really have one so close to the cells?

A stone scrapes against his cheek; it's round and smooth and it seems to be fastened on the mattress, and it's not a stone. And the cell is not a cell. Kouplan opens his eyes and stares at mocha upholstery.

She's put a blanket over him, with fringe that tickles his neck. He checks that he has all his clothes on, and he does. The wine has made his tongue thick like porridge. He turns onto his back and looks at Pernilla's ceiling.

"It was a bad idea to open that second bottle of wine," Pernilla says. "How are you feeling?"

How's he feeling? First and foremost happy that he hasn't really woken up in a jail cell. On the other hand, his mind and his body are not cooperating with each other.

"Fine," he says and raises himself on his elbow. "What time is it?"

It's nine thirty and Pernilla is making some sandwiches. His empty stomach growls at not receiving its usual oatmeal, or perhaps that's the wine, but his taste buds rejoice. She has some very good cheese, too, cheddar, and she's spreading butter on them as if she were making them for a child. The thought pinches his heart; it's almost ten and Julia is still out there.

What has he really found out from yesterday? Something, anything, that can excuse the wine? He chews a sandwich as he flips through his notebook to find musings about Pernilla's motives. At one spot, he's written: *Who is Julia?* He has to muddle through his mind to figure out what he meant.

"I'm making a few more; you can take them with you," Pernilla says.

Kouplan observes her. There's nothing evil in her soul, he feels. Something evasive is there, something that's hard to touch and it might be pain, but she can't make sandwiches like that and still be evil. So he puts a parenthesis around that question in his notebook and focuses on the other one.

"Yesterday I asked you about the year before you had Julia," he says. "But I don't believe you answered."

Pernilla doesn't get angry this time. Perhaps her brain is as wooly as his.

"What do you want to know?"

"The people you met. How you felt. If you had any other relationships."

Pernilla looks at her coffee cup. She sighs.

"I can't think of anything. But . . ."

"What is it?"

She shakes her head.

"Nothing. I can't remember anything specific. And, of course, that was before Julia. I mean, she didn't even exist then."

Kouplan looks at her intently, she can sense it and she knows he's paid attention to her *but*. But her thoughts stop there. She knows she's missing something, but it's like losing your vision right before getting a migraine. Something did happen before Julia was born, but she can't figure out what it is without falling.

Kouplan eats his fourth sandwich. She's noticed his thin body is always hungry. Just as she has to do when she has a migraine, Pernilla focuses on things other than what her eyes are trying to see.

"Didn't you mention your mother was a psychologist?"

Kouplan jerks, his hand holding the sandwich stops briefly in its tracks.

"Did I?" he replies. "Yes, she has a degree in psychology."

"And your father?"

"A professor."

He says this as if anyone can become a professor.

Pernilla has never even met one. She studies the somewhat curved nose of the son of a professor and imagines she sees something well read in his black eyebrows.

"Tell me about your life in . . ."

She stops. She's never asked him where he came from.

"Iran," Kouplan says.

He drinks an entire cup of coffee without saying more. Then he puts the cup on its saucer and he swallows an extra time.

"I didn't have a life in Iran," he says. "I had a childhood and a family. Then I had a time."

Pernilla listens and tries to understand the difference between a time and a life. It feels like the difference between what she knows and what she doesn't know.

"Then I came here," Kouplan says and she wonders what he's left out, but she doesn't ask. "And then I almost had a life. Yes, I had a life, in order to . . . but now I have a time again."

She understands enough to fill in his thought.

"And you're longing for a life."

". . . longing for a life."

Their eyes meet; she whose child is gone and he who needs a life. This thought makes her want to open another bottle of wine.

Instead, she says, "What are you going to do today?"

Kouplan says he's going to Hökarängen and to Globen and he'll be making a few phone calls. Pernilla forces herself to think this sounds good. It seems he has some clues. Then he asks about Thor.

"Don't freak out now," he says. "But is it possible that Thor is the father of your child?"

She has to laugh—she almost laughs out loud.

"No," she replies, shaking her head emphatically.

Thor is not Julia's father. She is almost completely sure of that.

Before he goes, she asks him if there's anything she can do right now. She's washed windows and there's not a single dirty dish in the house. She's taken deep breaths with Janus's paws resting on her stomach, she's hiccoughed from crying, and she's vomited in the toilet. Perhaps there's something better for her to do? Perhaps come with Kouplan?

"Just think," he says. "See if there's a photo anywhere or if you can remember anything that happened before Julia was born or when she was small. You can write down everything you're thinking."

He looks at her with those professor eyes, those psychologist eyes.

"And you can think back to that Monday."

He does not say *the day Julia disappeared*.

"Do you remember seeing a man with a large nose?"

Pernilla can only remember what she's already told him. That it was raining, that she had an umbrella. But perhaps, if she thinks about it, she could have seen a man with a somewhat large nose. Perhaps to the left, by the ticket office. She can remember trees that had lost their leaves in the fall. She can almost remember a man behind them, and if she remembers rightly, he could have had a large nose.

"But there was nothing remarkable about him," she says. "Otherwise, I would have thought about it."

"It wasn't anyone you would recognize," Kouplan says.

Of course it wouldn't be.

Kouplan gets off the bus at Gullmarsplan subway station. He's lost in thoughts about M.B., large noses, suspicious priests, and Pernilla's uncertainty, as she says who definitely is not Julia's father. Somehow, all of this must fit together. *Let's say,* he says to his brother in his head. *Let's say that we've decided to kidnap a specific child. There's some dark, hidden reason why we want to take her, but the mother would recognize us if we come too close, so what do we do? Well, we find someone who has experience in kidnapping people. Stockholm is a large city, but it's probably not crawling with experienced kidnappers, so we'd do the same thing as Rashid—ask around, find our most shady friends and drop hints to get a name. I doubt that there are all that many names in this city. And then how many hard-boiled kidnappers are there who've taken a blond girl of about seven? What do you think?*

Kouplan's brother does not answer, but then Kouplan's phone vibrates and right when he is about to answer, he sees a policeman heading straight toward him. His legs almost collapse beneath him and the policeman raises a hand and says in a deep voice, almost as if in slow motion:

"Hi, there, could you . . ."

It doesn't matter how much Kouplan trains his heart. It goes from zero to one hundred in a second, pumping blood to his legs that are the only things that can save him. Kouplan does the only—the most stupid thing that he can—rush into the crowd pouring out of the subway, slip through it like an eel heading upstream, run down the stairs to the subway trains. He can't feel his feet as he jumps onto the tracks on the other side of the elevator, stumbles and says a quick prayer to the God he does not believe in, lands centimeters from the contact rail and flies over three tracks at the same time. The officer is behind him or perhaps in front of him; the sounds around him are trains and the echoes of shouting human beings; his heart keeps pumping power to his legs until they can't take much more, until he finds himself back on the road. Nobody's calling out to him any longer, but he keeps running toward Globen, past the kiosk with the Kurd. Stockholm in October is a washed out gray curtain, as he crosses the bridge to Skärmarbrink, turns onto a bike path, and then sinks, a pulsating wreck, huddling behind a bush.

After ten minutes, nothing has moved. No uniforms appear in the distance between the houses and the street crossing, no police dogs or guards stuffed with adrenaline. Just rotting leaves beneath his hands, five cigarette butts, and an empty coffee cup before his eyes. It was just a warning. Kouplan releases the first deep breath he's taken since he stepped off the bus, feels how his lungs quiver. He

sits up on the rotting leaves and ducks his head away from
a branch. Pulls out his telephone—didn't it buzz a lifetime
ago?

It's Rashid. Kouplan calls the number on the screen as he
gets up from behind the bush and brushes off his clothes.
A black bird stares at him, confused.

"Rashid? Hi, it's Kouplan."

He doesn't mention the police. That would just keep
Rashid awake at night. Instead, he says he's been running
and that's why he's out of breath. Rashid asks if he's been
doing something stupid, but Kouplan replies he's been
doing something good.

"I'm helping someone out."

"And I'm helping you. A guy's coming to the grill this
afternoon. He's M.B.'s errand boy. He's supposed to pick
up something."

"For M.B.?"

"Don't know. Don't want to know. He'll be here at two."

Kouplan's phone shows 11:45.

CHAPTER 20

Kouplan's telephone shows 11:45, so he has time to go to Hökarängen. You have to think logically; you have to think that the errand boy can lead him to M.B. but perhaps neither of them will lead him to Julia. You have to also think that a kidnapper perhaps doesn't tell the truth to all the ticket agents he meets, Kouplan thinks, as he gets off the subway.

In Hökarängen, there are trees in one direction, apartment buildings in another, and in a third, there's a small center. Kouplan chooses the apartment buildings. They're located between cross streets and playgrounds with sandboxes. Empty, except for two children. The older brother is about five and the younger one is perhaps three. They're building sandcastles and don't notice Kouplan, but he stops. This is Sweden, with red rocking horses and scraggly city fir trees beside the corners of the buildings, but Kouplan sees himself and his brother. Someone opens a window on the fourth floor; a woman calls out in Arabic

and the older brother looks up. Answers: "We're coming!"
Kouplan's mother used to do the same thing; open the window and yell when food was ready. He walks to the door
as if he lives there and greets the children. *"Salaam alei-
kum."* The five-year-old looks at him, shy but courageous,
just like Kouplan's brother would have done. The three-
year-old hides behind him, a tiny boy behind his big
brother.

"Are you the only children around here?" Kouplan
asks.

The five-year-old measures him with his stare, hesitates
but then replies:

"There's a few more."

"Have any new kids shown up lately? The last few
days?"

"Like?"

"Some new girl, for instance. A Swedish girl who's
new here?"

The boy shakes his head. His little brother pulls
him by the hand to the stairs.

"Just the same kids as always," the boy explains as he
resists.

He'd always been the scared three-year-old. His brother
had always been the brave one. Kouplan doesn't want to
think about his brother's name, because at two o'clock,
he'll be spying on M.B.'s errand boy and there's no room
for feelings. But his brother had always been the brave one
and if Kouplan had room for feelings right now, he'd be

wondering if his brother was brave now, whether here on earth or in heaven.

Instead, he thinks about how the world is full of people who have disappeared. He looks around without a plan, walks along Lingvägen and Russinvägen without seeing anyone with a large nose or a blond six-year-old. He walks back to the newsstand and the grocery store and wonders how many of the people standing in line have had a person in their lives become lost. They all share a certain emptiness, all those people who have lost people. They all share a special emptiness.

Pernilla should never have taken out her old computer. It should have remained where it was, stuck in the back of the basement storage unit behind an exercise machine. That machine represents an alternative reality—defined stomach muscles that could have been; her computer signifies much the same.

But now it's in the living room and starts up slowly just like an old memory. She also has to haul up the screen, since she can't connect the computer to her laptop. The background shines at her like a wronged ghost. Other mothers have pictures of their children, mouths sticky with jam, on their computer screens. Pernilla has a picture of someone's hands. Once upon a time, she'd found the picture calming; today it made her nervous. She'd taken the picture herself. Was it Patrick's hands or Thor's? For a moment, it seemed as if they could reach out from the screen and she instinctively covers her breasts. She never should have taken out the computer, but she grabs the mouse and clicks on *Pictures*.

The thing was, Julia didn't like having her picture taken. Cameras made her panic. Or maybe it was Pernilla who was afraid of them? She remembers something all of a sudden. They were at Skansen and Julia was almost three. They were by themselves; they were walking past a friendly squirrel when a man approached them with a camera. Pernilla could still feel her panic and the fear that they'd discover Julia and take her away. She can still hear the anxiety in her voice as she asks Julia to turn away from the camera and run toward the old parish house. And Julia listened, as children always do when they realize that things are serious. And Julia ran.

She opens her laptop and writes down this memory. Not because it might help Kouplan, however much he may believe it would, but because it could help her. If only the picture around that time she could not remember would become as clear, perhaps she would be able to see into the empty space, whether she wanted to or not.

The first photographs are of herself and Jörgen. Jörgen was very much like Patrick, actually, just with hair dyed black and less strength. How in love she'd been and how awful that he had died. She also had black hair in the pictures—they'd shared home dye every month in order to save money. Jörgen appears most often on the screen— sometimes he'd set up the camera toward both of them for silly self-portraits. She looks into his blue eyes that no longer exist. She can feel his warm hand on her back; no, that's her dog Janus.

"Look here," she says. "If that hadn't happened . . . fourteen years ago. This guy would be your master."

Janus doesn't bother to look at the picture. He just lays his chin on Pernilla's lap and looks up at her, and his dog body moves with his breathing. Pernilla scratches his shaggy head with one hand while she clicks through with the other.

"And here's some from my former job. That guy wearing a tie, that's Perra, he wanted to sleep with me. That's only because I dyed my hair blond; that was after Jörgen. That woman with the low-cut dress, she was a real bitch; sorry, but she was."

There's a knot inside her, which, although it's not dissolving, hurts less the more she talks to Janus about old times. She tells him about the cherry blossoms in May 2004 and about the vacation in Gotland in 2006, shows him a crooked sunset and several more pictures of Patrick than of herself. There are fifty-seven pictures in the entire folder, less than five a year, and hardly any after Julia was born. There's not a single one of Julia.

Her heart sinks as she realizes this. She knows she's been careful, but at least three times she'd pressed the shutter to immortalize her beautiful child. She's absolutely sure she's done so—she can close her eyes and see a picture of her newborn Julia wrapped in a red-striped blanket. Another photograph should have shown Julia in a sun

hat standing on a stone path and a third should have had
her in her yellow pajamas. But they're not in the folder.
Someone has deleted them.

Errand boy. Both in Persian and in Swedish, the word
sounds like it describes a nimble youth, as thin as Kouplan
or even thinner, but the man Rashid has indicated as M.B.'s
errand boy is anything but. The seriousness of what's happening grabs Kouplan the second he nears the entrance
and sees the enormous back through the glass door of the
grill—the seriousness that appears when something, like a
train at full-speed or a mountain impossible to climb, is
right before you, greater than yourself.

   Kouplan walks inside, head down, two broken ear
buds in his ears. When the errand boy with his bulging
muscles glances in his direction, Kouplan nods as if he's
keeping time with a hip-hop beat. The errand boy soon
loses interest in him and takes the double portion of kebab that Azad hands him and starts eating, open-mouthed.
He sits down in the corner, so close that his right shoulder
almost touches Kouplan's left one. Across the table, there's
a white guy, perhaps Swedish, perhaps Polish, or maybe
from the Balkans. The men who own Rashid's apartment
also got him the dishwashing job, and perhaps this white
guy is one of them. The two men are talking, but Kouplan
can't hear what they're saying, although he can feel the vi-
brations of the errand boy's voice. In another life, he could
have been a baritone.

   If Kouplan's understanding of human beings has any-

thing to tell him, it's that the mumbling white guy isn't
M.B. M.B. has contacts and subordinates; M.B. is the one
who makes money on women, and he would never sit leaning forward like that. After eating half his kebab, the
white guy grabs a fistful of salt packets from the table, and
the errand boy does the exact same thing shortly
afterward—it's the most obvious transaction Kouplan has
ever seen. He concludes that neither of them is all that in-
telligent.

The tempting French fries are still on the thinner guy's
plate when the two of them get up to leave. Soon the food
will be scraped away into the fast food place's large garbage cans and there's nothing Kouplan can do to grab
them for himself in a normal, not obvious manner. He
slinks out a few seconds after the errand boy and sees that
the white guy has already disappeared. The huge back is
moving toward Medborgarplatsen and Kouplan prays for
two things over and over again: *Don't turn around. Don't
take a taxi.*

He's the child of a professor and a psychologist, he
thinks, as he shadows the errand boy past the cafés of Södermalm. It's unreal how he, born in a hot country to
parents with double degrees, is now following a mountain
of muscle while avoiding the police like a criminal in this
October chill of Stockholm. All it would take is the errand
boy being followed by yet someone else so that he, himself,
would turn into a target for unimagined criminals. He
won't be able to ask the police for help—he'd be nothing
more than a pimple between two implacable thumbnails.

Mâmân, he thinks, *Allah, Bâbâ, brother*. But all he has is himself and his own body. He follows the errand boy down into the subway and the earth closes above them.

They return to the surface in Akalla. Three stations earlier, they'd passed Kouplan's home and he felt a sting of longing for a shower. Now he has neither the time to think about his own bathroom, or Pernilla's, which he should have taken advantage of, because the massive errand boy takes the escalator up two steps at a time and heads for the light of Akalla. Kouplan runs up as fast as he dares; he can't do the same thing as the errand boy without drawing attention to himself. At the entrance, he stands there at a loss until he catches sight of a spot of shining black and realizes it's the errand boy's jacket. He's swaggering along, greeting the boys in front of the newsstand with a nod. Here the errand boy is a king; he strides across the street and shoves a door open with his shoulder. Kouplan glances up at the sign: a gym.

The errand boy is in the gym for an hour and a half. After the first twenty-five minutes have gone by, Kouplan heads somewhere to grab a hamburger to keep from fainting, and then spends the next sixty minutes worrying that the errand boy is still in the gym. Still, who can look like that if you're only at the gym fifteen minutes a day? When the man comes out again, he's carrying a gym bag over his shoulder. This means he must have been there that morning and left it there and that means he works out twice a day. Kouplan shudders—his sixty push-ups every morning are nothing in comparison.

If Kouplan had been working out, then taken the subway to slip secrets via salt packets at a grill, eaten kebab, and then worked out a second time, he'd finish the day by going home. Therefore, he's fairly sure that the building the errand boy walks into is, as Thor the priest would put it, his own humble abode. The errand boy's humble abode is a thirteen-story apartment building with brown walls and hundreds of anonymous windows. Kouplan is too far behind to have any chance of sticking his foot in the door, which closes behind the errand boy to leave Kouplan outside. He says a quick prayer to Allah, who reasonably should not even listen to him since his faith is fairly selective, but he receives assistance this time: The lock is broken. He hurries to the elevator and watches the numbers on the digital screen shift slowly to nine, ten, eleven, and then stop at twelve. Five minutes later, Kouplan takes the same ride up.

All the doors have peepholes, so Kouplan just looks at all the nameplates, puts them into his memory, and goes back to the elevator. He rides to the thirteenth floor, tests the door to the fire escape and slinks into the stairwell. The thirteenth floor seems dusty and unused; on the twelfth floor, he sees dirty footprints on the landing. In the groove by the stairs, there are butts from hand-rolled cigarettes and one unopened condom. He sits on the edge of the first step and exhales. The stairwell could use some air. He takes out his notebook and writes down everything he knows about the errand boy. Or whatever he should call him. Most of the names on the twelfth floor were Chinese;

the others were Nilsson, Chavez, and Papadakis. The errand boy could be one of these three, but Kouplan makes an educated guess that his name is Chavez. Then he carefully opens the metal door that leads to the twelfth floor.

The rectangular length of nothing that binds Nilsson, Chavez, and Papadakis with the Chinese is empty and just as quiet as wooden doors with peepholes would allow. Kouplan looks down at the condom lying in the gap beneath the door. *Ultimate protection* it says on the wrapper and Kouplan prays this is true. He withdraws back into the stairwell, leaving a gap of sallow light. From the first step, with his head against the stone-colored wall, he has an inch-wide perfect view of the elevators.

CHAPTER 21

Adults thunder like moose on the stairs. Before they'd even start running, they're on the next flight of stairs, and a child doesn't have a chance to be quicker. A child, for instance, a girl, won't be able to get more than half a flight away, even if she rushes out the moment the man unlocks the door. She's been counting, felt in her body how fast she can run, and did her best to be truthful. She knows that men can run faster if they really want to.

She has figured out that she is on the fourth floor. She's figured this out because there is a building on the other side of the street and the window across from her is the fourth from the ground. She's just a child, but she's not stupid and she knows how to count. And she can open windows.

In order to get to the latch, she has to climb on the dresser and pull with all her might. Finally, the clasp loosens along with two layers of paint, and she pushes at the window, first carefully and then as hard as she can. At first, it seems like the window is stuck, but all of a sudden, the paint gives and the window opens with such speed that she loses her balance. For one frightful second, she's staring right down four floors and sees the street below. She's holding to the window latch and pulls herself back inside with her feet, and she doesn't breathe until she's back inside. Her lungs pump out her fear and she feels her blood humming like bumblebees in her hands and feet. In one way, she feels more alive than she has during the past few days.

Once she catches her breath, she sticks her head out the window. It's just as far to the ground as before, but her feet are now anchored on the floor. On the sidewalk below, people are walking past as small as beetles. Between them cars stop and go, stop and go. Behind the cars, there are signs that shine all through the night. She's seen them before, but they are clearer now that the window is open.

"A-P-O-T-E-K," she spells aloud. "G-A-L-L-E-R-I."

She thinks the first place must be one where people buy medicine. She has no idea what the other sign means. But perhaps the people who sell medicine would care about little girls.

She waits until a person in a white coat comes out of the apothecary. That person, a white beetle, brings her hand to her mouth and soon smoke comes out. Now or never.

She stares right at that beetle person, opens her mouth and screams as loud as she can. Since she first saw that man who called himself her real father, she's screaming for help so loudly that it echoes from the building wall across the street, and the people react, but not with alarms or with police cars with sirens on. Instead, they seem hesitant or appear irritated. She yells that she's here, up here, UP HERE and that they've taken her, but nobody is glancing upward at the fourth floor and all of a sudden the locked door flies open.

It's not the man who calls himself her real father, but the other one. He doesn't yell, but he growls and mutters angrily as he slams the window closed. Then he grabs her by the hair, her hair that hurts even when her mother tries to comb it, especially the thin strands by her neck. He grabs it and lifts her straight up and it hurts so much, tears come to her eyes. She can feel the strands of hair pulling off her scalp, but most of them hold as he carries her across the room. He screams at her the entire time and she doesn't understand much besides that she was not allowed to yell to the people on the street below. He could have dropped her on the bed, but instead he drops her on the floor. From below, he appears as large and mighty as a monster truck, and his face is the ugliest she has ever seen. Before he leaves, he spits on her. He's aiming for her face but it lands on her neck. She wipes it off once he's gone and it smells rank and pungent and she smears it on the door.

Then she lies on the bed for a while. Her scalp throbs and aches. She feels it to see if she's lost much hair, but that doesn't seem to be the case. She looks up at the ceiling and presses on her scalp, which starts to feel swollen after a time. She sighs and thinks about her mother. In the evenings, she can remember how her mother would hug her and make their supper, how they'd laugh at TV shows or do a puzzle. But during the days, the guilt takes over. Her mother had told her clearly what she should do if someone tried to kidnap her. *Yell and run*, her mother had said, and her voice echoes over and over: *Yell and run*. But she didn't yell and she hadn't run, so she let her own mother down. If she thinks about it too much, she starts to cry.

CHAPTER 22

Kouplan's bony rump chafes on the stone stairs that, in case of fire, would save the inhabitants of the Sibelius building. His neck has stiffened at a three-quarters angle, and, although he's waking up, he feels like he hasn't slept. He's been sitting all night in the same position, dozing and half-dreaming of falling down twelve flights of stairs and landing in ice-cold jail cells, waking from his cell phone reminder that his battery is low and from the rumbling in his stomach. It hasn't been a whole night, actually, as it's just four thirty in the morning when the first rattle of a door lock starts. It's a Chinese woman of about forty, who yawns mightily while the elevator heads up through its shaft. Kouplan checks the time.

By six a.m., he's wondering what he's doing here. If Julia's kidnapper had headed to Hökarängen, why is he sitting in a really cold staircase in Akalla and staring at the elevator door? If Patrick acts like he's not Julia's father and Thor reacts with such unconcern when hearing about her disappearance, why isn't he shadowing them instead? His only answer is unsatisfactory: gut feeling.

By seven, the rest of the building is waking up. The elevator is working several times every hour, even though it is a Sunday. Two more Chinese women head down from the twelfth floor, and once the elevator heads up to the thirteenth floor. Three hours later, Chavez appears.

It's a shock when Chavez is actually standing there, taking up the entire gap that Kouplan has been staring through. First Kouplan's legs don't obey him, but he forces them to move. He jogs down two flights of stairs as he counts the seconds. On the tenth floor, he pushes the door open and throws himself at the elevator button. He didn't need to be in such a hurry. The elevator is still heading up from the seventh floor and he has time to catch his breath. Before the elevator has time to reach the twelfth floor and turn around, a family with children all dressed up to go to church has joined him. He lets them enter the elevator before him as a buffer between him and the errand boy Chavez.

The sun pokes him in the eyes. It's a sunny day, especially bright for someone who has been sitting for sixteen hours in a drab stairwell. Kouplan blinks until he can see properly; he breathes in the fresh air as if it were a good but insufficient breakfast and follows Chavez, who does not seem to be in much of a hurry. The sign in the subway shows eight minutes until the next train, so Kouplan has enough time to buy a hardtack sandwich from the machine. He looks away as he drops the coins in—for that amount of money he could buy half a box of hardtack at the supermarket. But there's value in not fainting.

At the Central Station, he keeps behind Chavez, as far back as he can, so that he's actually following the top of a haircut. He should have changed his clothes, he thinks, because how long can a person be shadowed without realizing that the skinny guy in the brown jacket is starting to seem familiar?

At Slussen, Chavez changes to Bus Number 3. Chavez sits all the way in the back, so Kouplan sits up front. Each time the bus stops, he can glance in the rearview mirror, and at Renstierna street, it's Chavez's massive body that exits the rear bus door. When he gets up to leave at the same stop, he notices that Chavez is looking both ways, just like Kouplan does when he wants to avoid the police. Therefore, he stays on the bus, now sitting far in the back and watching Chavez through the dirtiest back window he's ever seen. At the next stop, he hops off, crosses the street and saunters toward the building that has just swallowed Chavez. The door is locked and Chavez has disappeared.

He needs to get a pair of binoculars, he thinks, once he's sat down at the restaurant across the street. A waitress asks him what he wants and he asks for the menu. He really could use a pair of binoculars that could see into each room and reveal who Chavez has come to meet. Instead, he only has his own set of peering eyes, and, behind them, the beginnings of a headache.

"Have you decided?" the persistent waitress asks and he forces himself to smile as he shakes his head.

At least the sun is in the right direction, and behind one of the windows, there's movement. Third floor, the side next to Vita Hill. Perhaps he's imagining things, but it appears to be Chavez's silhouette he sees inside. It's been in front of his eyes for two days, so he's pretty sure he recognizes it.

"My boss says you have to order something if you want to stay," the waitress declares. Her voice is hostile.

Kouplan can imagine how he appears. It's been two days since he's taken a shower and if he were the waitress's boss, he'd also have his concerns.

"I'm sorry," he says as he hands her the unopened menu. "There's nothing here that I'm not allergic to."

He gets up and leaves, the waitress behind him exclaiming: "You can't be allergic to everything!" and walks out to go around the corner to Vita Hill. From the stairs up the hill, he can see many windows of the same apartment and it seems to him that there's a tall, male figure next to the man who must be Chavez. Then he realizes how badly he needs to pee.

Some guys wake up in other people's stairwells and decide to take a piss right there. It's not their stairwell and they do need to pee. Then there's the larger group of guys that could go pee behind a bush at Vita Hill Park, at least if things are really pressing. Kouplan wishes he belonged to at least one of those groups, but he doesn't. He presses his thighs together in an especially ridiculous way, while he also tries to concentrate on discovering important clues through a window twenty meters away. Finally, he has to capitulate and he runs down the wooden stairs and into a café. "PleaseletmeusethebathroombeforeIpeealloverthe-floor," he says, and it's the threat and perhaps the desperation in his voice, but the guy behind the counter waves him toward the door for the bathroom, and behind it is thirty seconds of absolute heaven.

Once he's run back up the stairs at Vita Hill, Chavez's silhouette in the window is gone. The other man is standing in yellow light, turned toward what might be a kitchen counter. Perhaps he's weighing substances. Or making mac and cheese. Kouplan glances down toward Skånegatan, penetrating the window across the street. If Chavez is still in the apartment, he'd appear in one or the other window eventually. If a man is making mac and cheese for a little girl, you'd eventually see a small shadow move. Neither thing happens.

It's only two days before November starts and the wooden stairs are dry but cold. As Kouplan sits, it doesn't take long before a winter chill starts moving up through his jeans and onto his thin limbs. He's now spent twenty-four hours on stairs and his stomach is screaming about the lone hardtack sandwich. He leans against the railing as he observes the man in the yellow kitchen. He's not ready to leave yet.

There's a connection, he feels after a half an hour of

observation, between himself and the man in the kitchen. The connection is that the man is walking around his apartment and Kouplan is watching him walk around his apartment. It's the same kind of attachment a stalker has to his victims. The simile swirls in a meaningless way through his mind and is broken by an absolutely true picture of his father. Kouplan is little and his father is twice as big. "*Sabr talx ast, valikan bar-e širin dārad,*" his father is saying. "Patience is bitter, but its fruit is sweet." Perhaps he means that waiting for the man in the apartment to do something is leading somewhere or he means Kouplan's entire existence. But now all Kouplan can think of is sweet fruit. Apricots, plums, grapes, melons. The feeling of soft fruit skin breaking between his teeth, the juice running down his chin if you don't slurp it in immediately. Then kebab, the first bite of one with *everything on it*. Then *ghejme badenjan* stew with extra lamb. Once his dreams have gone to fish sticks and mashed potatoes, he realizes he's gone too far. Chavez is not appearing in the apartment, in the entrance, or on the street. Through the window, there's not one single strand of a little girl's hair. Before Kouplan leaves, he goes to the entrance of the building and finds the name of the man: F. Karlsson.

On the subway back, he summarizes his day in his notebook. First he's writing in Persian and then in Swedish: *Nineteen hours observation and hungry like hell.*

There's something special about hunger. Along with the need for peeing and the need for sleep, it overrides all the other needs one can have. That's what people call the Maslow stages of need. As he shovels oatmeal into his mouth, he can hear his mother telling him about Maslow in his mind. "Bodily needs come first," she explains. "Next comes the need for security." Kouplan makes another portion of oatmeal and he can hear his father repeat the proverb. It's as if his hunger is calling them back. He thinks one thought halfway through, wondering how they are. If he completes the thought, he will have to think that his mother must be thinking the same about him and his brother, and he can't face that. His mother would say that it's not healthy.

Once his stomach is full of oatmeal, he opens his notebook. He rereads his observations and realizes that nineteen hours of work have not brought him any closer to Julia. It's been two weeks since she disappeared, and a six-year-old is somewhere right now, at this very moment when Kouplan has finished scraping the last of his oatmeal from his bowl, right *now*, frightened because of where she's ended up.

Either that, or a six-year-old body is somewhere.

Either that, or Pernilla is lying.

CHAPTER 23

It sounds crazy, but it's true: Someone has erased every trace of Julia. There hadn't been many, and the ones that had existed had not been easy to find, but someone had found every last one of them and destroyed them. After Pernilla had not been able to find any traces of photos in her old computer, she'd gone through her entire apartment filled with fear. A chill spread in her body as she realized that there was not a single piece of evidence to show that Julia was hers—her precautions had backfired and someone had committed the perfect crime.

Who would have known that she had some pictures of Julia in an old, bulky computer in the basement storage space? Who knew that she had a lock of hair in an old, red box? She was the only one, right? And—her thoughts bother her and then scare her—and Julia. Julia, who giggled when she cut off a lock of hair. Julia, who went with her to the basement when she brought down her old computer.

She can't explain why she started to think about Thor.

He would never kidnap a child, but perhaps, if he thought he was helping, he would ask Julia some questions. Julia is shy, but kind and, above all, just six. Six-year-olds trust people—it's part and parcel of their age. But he would never kidnap a child, she repeats to herself.

"I'm paying you to find Julia," Pernilla says testily to Kouplan.

They're walking from Gullmarsplan to Globen. Again. She hates the walkway beneath the bridge; she hates the Subway and the Greek restaurant.

"I will find Julia," he says. "But I need you for this."

"That's not it. I'm just paying you to find her, okay?"

"What's wrong?"

He stops to look at her, his fine brown eyes questioning. His entire body is ready, Pernilla thinks. He seems to be calm, but inside he is ready for anything. Even for what she's going to say.

"I only had three pictures of Julia," she says. "And one lock of hair in a box. I had them in the apartment and in my storage unit, but they've disappeared."

He's silent; his forehead wrinkles slightly.

"So she's completely gone now?" he asks.

She exhales, because he believes her.

He could disappear like that, Kouplan thinks. If something happened to him now, he'd cease to exist completely. Just like Julia, there's nothing of him but a body. It's a risky way to live.

"Didn't you ever think of it?"

The question had been on his tongue for so long that it had to come out.

"All the time," Pernilla replies. "But they were threatening to take her when she was still inside me. I couldn't let them. And if I showed up, say, two years later with an unregistered child . . . guess who would have been an incompetent mother."

"Yes, well . . . that is . . . would she . . . would you have homeschooled her, or what? And what if she'd gotten seriously ill?"

Pernilla's eyes fill with tears.

"Don't you believe I'd been thinking about all that? Don't you believe that's exactly what I'd been worrying about all along?"

She's practically spitting it out and he lays an arm on her shoulder, not thinking about it for the first time, and she doesn't push him away. He wants to ask: *Why were you so afraid that someone would take her? What made you think this way? Every detail is important.* He wants to say this, but her shoulders are shaking.

"Now we keep going," he says. "We'll find her."

Today, Globen is the right place to be if you're looking for a girl. An entire archipelago of them fills the square and there are festival tents, sleeping bags, and teddy bears. The girls inhabiting the space ought to be in school, but by their T-shirts, it's easy to tell that Justin Bieber is a greater need on their Maslow scale. There are hundreds of them.

"Don't think about them," Kouplan says to Pernilla. "Close your eyes."

Pernilla obeys. She's standing beside him like a normal Swedish mother, but just moments away from pure panic. He watches her push it away; he sees the vibrating abyss behind her eyelids.

"First take a deep breath."

About ten girls are screaming from excitement—apparently for no reason—not too far from them. Pernilla inhales. Kouplan observes the thin lines around her mouth.

"And out again. And then think about that day, but earlier. Did you talk to anyone?"

"On the subway?"

"Or before then. At home. Did you speak to someone on the phone or did you meet someone? How about the day before?"

The girls behind Pernilla are practicing some invented choreography to their phones and writing *Belieber* on each other's foreheads. Pernilla breathes in, breathes out.

"I don't remember anything on that day. But on Sunday, we went for a walk."

"You and Julia?"

"No, Janus. Julia stayed at home."

He made a mental note. Julia stayed at home. Why?

"And you were talking to someone?"

"There was a guy with another mutt."

She suddenly opens her eyes.

"Is any of this important?"

"Shut your eyes. A guy who also had a mutt. Had you seen him before?"

"A few times. We often walk the same route. We say hi."

He sees that the panic leaves her eyes and gives way to something else. Perhaps she's focusing.

"Had he ever met Julia?"

She leaves time to think and then replies:

"No, I don't think so. No, I only saw him when I was alone with the dog. I think she was outside with me once, but she was on the playground. They never met."

Kouplan imagines he's a man with a dog.

"Perhaps he's afraid of children," he says. "Perhaps he only says hi when he sees you're alone."

When Pernilla closes her eyes, he can see everything in her face. She's not able to control it as much; he can see her doubt before she even says the words.

"I was thinking along the same lines."

I'm getting paid to believe her, he thinks as they walk toward Skärmarbrink. They're walking along the same route that a man with a large nose had walked with a young girl two weeks ago, and he's no longer sure that he's part of that situation. He has something else going on—that Pernilla isn't telling him everything. But he's getting paid to believe her.

"Did she often stay home when you went out with Janus?" he asks.

"More and more often. I think maybe because she was older or maybe she was getting tired of walking the dog, even though she loved him so much at first. But I don't know . . . do you think children can get depressed?"

Kouplan had been crowded on refugee buses and lived in residences for asylum seekers; he'd been rejected along with entire families and he'd seen five people sharing one bed. If children can get depressed?

"You could say . . . you could say that Julia was a hidden child, couldn't you?"

Pernilla's face was that of a parent's conscience.

"But I tried to give her everything. Stimulating activities . . . and . . . I mean, we went to the library, did some bead mosaics . . ."

Kouplan asks, "Do you still have them?"

"Yeah, why?"

Kouplan doesn't say anything, but he's thinking: Someone has taken photos and a lock of hair but left bead mosaic pictures. Someone was strategic, or perhaps just cruel. They'd come to the bridge over the train tracks. He stops and lowers his voice.

"Is there anyone who does not like you?"

She gives a dry laugh.

"Besides Patrick?"

Kouplan leans against the fence and looks down onto the tracks. The train to Farsta, with its striped roof and glowing signs, thunders below them. He thinks about directions, about clues.

"Someone who wants to hurt you," he says. "Someone who would go so far as to take your child."

Pernilla stands beside him. The train to Farsta

disappears around the corner, leaving nothing but vibrating rails.

"Apparently."

Kouplan has two feelings that don't match. The first feeling tells him that someone who needed a child saw an opportunity and kidnapped Julia. The other one tells him that Julia's disappearance is connected to Pernilla somehow. Or with Julia herself. How long can a child remain hidden? What does a child hide within itself when it is hidden? What does the child long for? What is it receptive to? And he thinks about points of intersection.

A point of intersection happens when one graph meets another graph. It can illustrate the ultimate investment sum or the most profitable size of a pizza carton. And you could also say that it happens when a lost fish meets a hungry crocodile. And so if a child is frustrated enough at being hidden and tied to its mother and there's an adult in great need of a child . . .

If you have two equations with two unknown factors, there are three methods of finding out how they intersect. Although this is true for mathematics, these former words of his old math teacher make Kouplan feel that the answer is much closer. His two feelings can both be true, once he figures out how they intersect.

He can also be completely wrong.

A real policeman would never bring a distraught mother on an aimless walk through a suburb on the south side of the city. Right now he can only choose between M.B. and Pernilla, and he can't get Pernilla to talk if she's not with him. The train tracks are now silent and empty except for two ragged pigeons pecking at invisible food. Pernilla replies to a question he hasn't asked.

"Some things are murky. I don't remember them so clearly."

Kouplan thinks she's working her way to something important, so he focuses on the birds as he quietly says:

"What kind of things?"

"When you ask me questions, it's like I can't remember. I try to, but it's like my brain doesn't want to bring me the answers."

"So you can't remember details, like what color or what time and the like?"

She shakes her head.

"No, it's like I can't remember how everything fits together. I think about a day, such as Sunday two weeks ago. I know Julia wasn't with me at the park, but I can't remember when I got home. And it's the same thing for longer stretches of time, like when you asked me about the year before Julia was born."

A man walks past them. His nose is distressingly small. Kouplan thinks that memory works like that for everybody. You don't remember when you get home. You don't remember every person you've ever met.

"Only witnesses on TV remember everything."

"But I don't think other people are like me."

Her voice transitions—truth is seeping into the air

around them. If this is true—if Pernilla has memory black-outs she can't explain . . .

"A memory loss like after taking drugs?" he asks.

She shakes her head. "No, I don't take drugs."

Kouplan reflects on the two bottles of wine they drank last Friday. On the other hand, the bottles were dusty. He thinks about people who drug other people.

"I don't know if it's shock," Pernilla says.

Kouplan thinks about people who take control over other people's lives.

"Does anyone else have keys to your apartment?"

Pernilla shakes her head.

"Only my landlord. Kouplan, I can't take much more of this. I'm starting to see Julia behind every single bush."

Kouplan shivers and realizes Pernilla is right. She should not be out here with him.

"I'm going to keep going on my own," he says. "I'm going to get in touch with my contacts and see if they've found out anything more. Then there's another place I want to check out."

"I wish I could help. I'm going crazy."

"Have you written down things like I asked you to? Anything you remember might be useful."

"At least five pages."

"Keep writing. If I don't find Julia by tomorrow, I'll drop by and pick it up."

"Nothing I write is going to help."

Probably not help me, Kouplan thinks. *But it might*

help you in the long run. He'd told her about finding Julia by tomorrow just to give her hope. A child who has been missing for longer than two weeks is probably not alive.

"Trust me," he says.

CHAPTER 24

Her mother had forgotten to tell her one thing when she warned her about getting kidnapped. She forgot to tell her what to do if she had been kidnapped.

Now all she has is her own mind and the only way out is through the window. She walks over to it and unlatches the latch the growling man had shut. She thinks about Rapunzel who let down her golden hair. Her own hair only reaches the windowsill. There's no rope in the room, and if there were, it probably wouldn't reach down all four floors. She thinks about a TV show, how the characters tied sheets together. The bed in this room doesn't have any.

She's tried to count the days. She could think of five, but she's not sure if she's mixing them up. She doesn't know if yesterday was day number five or if it was the day before yesterday. She can't count how many times she's cried, or the nights where she lay awake staring at the black stripes on the curtains. She can count the men, however.

There are three of them.

The second man has an accent, which means he has a different language and can't speak hers so well. He takes care of "the girls" and brings them food from fast food places. "The girls": That's her and the two grown-ups from Poland. They speak Polish with each other and live in the room next door. At first, she wished she could stay with them, because they were nice to her even if they didn't understand her. They combed her hair and kissed her on the cheeks. But then she noticed that there were strange noises coming from their rooms: banging and moaning. The second man said that's when they had "visitors." In a few days, he told her, she'd also get "visits" and the most important thing for her to do was to keep quiet.

The third man didn't say anything at all, at least not to her. But he used English when he talked to the other two. She recognized the words *yes, no,* and *fuck*. He has hair in his ears and his nose looks like an enormous potato. She doesn't like any of them, but if she could choose which one she hated the most, she'd choose him.

The first man is the one who said he was her real father. He's coming in the room now as she is standing with her head out the window.

"You can't open the window," he says.

He says this like it's a recommendation, but she knows it's an order. Maybe even a threat. She quietly shuts the window and latches it properly.

"That's better."

He sits down on the bed without sheets. She's slept in

it for at least five nights and in a way it's hers and she doesn't like his rump on it.

"You're not my father," she whispers so silently that nobody should be able to hear it. She hasn't even really moved her lips. But he hears it.

"Stop making a fool out of yourself," he says. "You're a big girl now. You should get used to the situation."

She's curious, almost against her will. She knows he's lying. She just knows. But if he wasn't . . .

"I've talked to your mother. Come here!"

He pats the bed next to him, but she remains standing by the window. He probably didn't talk to her mother. Definitely not.

"I don't know if she ever told you that you were too much for her to handle."

He furrows his forehead as if he cares, as if he knows about her mother. Her insides turn cold. She doesn't want to remember that her mother had actually used almost those same words.

"So we decided that I'd have you from now on. She's had you for so long. It's difficult to have a child like you for such a long time. Aren't you going to come and sit down?"

He pats the bed again. She shakes her head and he forces a laugh.

"There you go. You don't do what people tell you to do. I can see why she doesn't want you anymore."

She mumbles a reply. She wants to keep it behind her lips, inside her mouth. But he hears everything.

"Speak up! What did you say?"

She has to open her mouth and give him the words she wants to keep.

"My mother loves me."

He nods sadly as he looks right at her.

"Yes, she used to love you, yes. But now she doesn't want you anymore. Stop arguing and come and sit down. I don't bite."

His voice is as hard as a monster's and it forces her. She lets go of the windowsill and walks over the floor to sit on the very edge of the bed.

"Now we understand each other," he says. "Next time you will do as I say immediately. So that I also don't get tired of having you around."

He puts a heavy hand on her shoulder, tries to pet her back in a fatherly way. Her back hates him through her sweater.

"Say, 'Yes, father.'"

All he does is tell lies, this man who says he's her real father. Everything he says is the opposite of the truth, so her answers can also be the opposite of the truth. He pinches her neck when she doesn't answer right away.

No, not-father.

"Yes, father."

CHAPTER 25

Kouplan feels he's missed something.

He thought he'd be so good at this. All he'd need was a case and he'd be the best brain in the world again, the person he was before he fled, the person his brother had made him feel he was. But his life is clouding his brain and although it's good sometimes to focus on something else, his total concentration makes him fear for his life. Just one second of distraction at the wrong time would be all that's needed. There's barbed wire around his reasoning and he can't figure it out. It's like Pernilla said: "It's as if my brain doesn't want to answer."

He's back in Akalla. Not because his clues have led him there, but because he can't think of anything else to do. He's already combed through Hökarängen and it would be a complete waste of time to hope for some luck there. He has no reason to visit Pernilla's ex-husband a second time and Thor has already come as close to breaking his professional confidentiality as he could. *I could question him again*, Kouplan thinks. *I could keep poking at him to see what might show through Thor's silences.* Just then the Sibeliusgången door opens and the enormous Chavez steps out.

Chavez is carrying his gym bag and heads straight for the gym. Kouplan follows at a safe distance and stops about fifty meters away when Chavez walks into the building. Then it's hard—all this standing around. If it were the middle of summer, it wouldn't be so bad. You can casually sit on a bench for hours, but at the end of October, that wouldn't seem normal at all. Kouplan leans against a wall and tries to look like a druggie waiting for his dealer. He squats but immediately thinks he looks like a homeless illegal immigrant, so he quickly stands back up. Finally, he takes out his phone, head down, as if he's in the middle of reading something extremely interesting. He moves his finger over his Ericsson T610 as if it could pick up the newspaper app, play Angry Birds, and check his mail. If someone walks past, he'd look like he was doing just that. The screen shines at him with the absolutely latest color circa 2003, say Telc2/Comviq with 128×160 pixels.

Fifty-five minutes later, Chavez comes out, now without his bag. Without looking, he crosses the street, heading in the direction of the subway station, as he shakes a plastic water bottle and then drinks as he heads to the subway station. He pulls out his card and walks underground. It's easy to shadow him here. Chavez is only nervously alert in the city. Kouplan reminds himself: *You're more vulnerable when you feel secure.*

They ride to Maria Square, the two of them, which ne-
cessitates changing trains. Twice Kouplan has to get out
of a car at the same time as Chavez and both times he has
to look as insignificant and unconcerned as he possibly
can. Luckily, he's had some practice in this art.

Maria Square is probably the most unpleasant corner of Stockholm. Small cafés and shops for sewing sup-
plies edge Hornsgatan. The cafés pull in young people,
huddled in winter parkas and eager for coffee. As the
street goes farther north, the shops transform into bou-
tiques and the side streets become more spruced up. At
the summit of the hill, the view is magnificent. But next
to the subway, by Thorkell Knutssonsgatan, there is a police station.

It's probable Chavez feels the same way about the
police station as Kouplan does, because he picks the far-
thest exit and then detours around before going on to his
real goal. At the entrance, he looks around quickly, and
Kouplan glances away into one of the side streets. When
he dares to look back, Chavez is gone. But he's sure that
he's gone into the building.

The street is about twenty feet wide. There's an apothecary and a gallery along one side. If he stands in front of
them and looks up at the windows, he'll be too visible, but
if he goes inside, he'll be unable to keep watch. Chavez
could exit the building at any time and spot the young man
from the elevator. At any time, a policeman could come by
and ask Kouplan for his identification. And there are only

two directions to run. He walks by the entrances as a normal person and then he stops and pulls out his phone as if he's just gotten a text message. Quickly glances at the windows, but sees nothing moving. Keeps walking, like an everyday citizen, and steps into the apothecary to warm up a bit. Most detective work these days goes on over the Internet, he'd read during his first days as a detective, but he hadn't been doing much of that.

Chavez buys snuff. He spits as he crosses the street. He spits on the sidewalk. He almost spits on a dog. *Do anabolic steroids affect saliva production?* Chavez makes phone calls. First to his barber to get an appointment and then to a colleague or friend—hard to tell. Kouplan hears snatches of the conversation: "What you up to?" and "Saw the boss just now, it . . ." and "Yeah, yeah, yeah." Kouplan scribbles everything down. The appointment could be code. *The boss*. That may be significant. That's all he catches.

Chavez spits on another crosswalk and looks back over his shoulder. Kouplan shivers as he judges the ratio between their respective muscle masses, three to one. He slips into a hole-in-the-wall convenience store, which is an absolutely stupid thing to do. He hears his brother: *Never go in anywhere unless you're positive there's a back door.* He's hoping that Chavez will keep going past the Italian restaurant and the electronics shop, but no, Chavez doesn't. He turns around. Kouplan sees this between the plastic letters on the shop door and he can read the guarded expression on Chavez's face. He's walking back slowly to this shop without a back door. *Think quickly! Think like the time at the border!*

The bell jingles and Chavez fills up the doorway as if the sun had suddenly suffered a total eclipse. Now three people are filling a space of less than ten square feet. Lottery ticket machines line the walls. Through sheer willpower, Kouplan faces the counter. His back and thin neck are turned on Chavez, much softer than anything Chavez could pound at the gym.

"Is that raspberry flavor?" Kouplan says in the highest voice he can manage while pointing at a display of lollipops.

The girl behind the counter glances first at Kouplan and then at Chavez. Even a stone could feel the tension in the room. She shakes her head slowly.

"Sorry, it's cherry."

"Oh, I hate cherry. Well, I'll take one of those instead." He points to the raspberry vines. Behind him is three hundred pounds of criminal steroids and here he is, buying candy.

"And a pack of cigarettes for my dad," he says, giving the girl a testing look.

It works.

"Do you have an ID?" she asks.

"It's not for me—it's for my dad."

"Well, then he has to come and buy them himself."

The shadow behind him eases away and cold autumn

air swirls in as Chavez heads out the door. The girl behind the counter gives Kouplan a meaningful look.

"That's one huge guy," she says.

Kouplan shrugs his shoulders and tries to look like the cheeky twelve-year-old he's playing. His soprano voice cheeps:

"What guy?"

His brother would be proud of him. First of all, because he's still alive. Second, he has survived by using one of his weak points. Not everyone has a voice that can sound like a middle-grader's. Not everyone looks like Darin's younger brother. You can get angry at your genetics or you can use them to your advantage.

His intelligence has let him figure out something else. *The boss.* He flips back to the address. He can keep following Chavez and count how often he spits, sure. But most detective work is done on the Internet.

Back in his room, he turns on his computer. It starts as slowly as a reluctant steam locomotive. It takes a few minutes before the Windows logo appears.

Somebody knocks at Kouplan's door. If Regina wants something, she usually waits until he comes into the kitchen and also this knocking is weak, about hip high. He gets up and opens his door.

"Hello, Liam."

Liam looks up at him. He has long, pale eyelashes and something important to say. But he can't get it out.

Kouplan says, "Do you want something?"

"Yeah, do you know what day it is tomorrow?"

Kouplan knows. Tomorrow is exactly one month and one year until he is allowed to ask for asylum again. If the rules don't change in the meantime.

"It's the first of November."

"But do you know what *day* it is?"

Apparently not.

"No, I don't."

"It's my birthday!"

Liam breaks out in the kind of smile that only a child can give the day before a birthday.

"Oh!" Kouplan adds, "That's great."

"I thought you'd want to know," Liam says as he kicks at the floor. "So you don't see everyone else with presents but you don't have one for me."

"That would be embarrassing," Kouplan agrees with a smile.

Liam isn't listening. He's already running back to the living room, singing a little song he's making up about his birthday. "November first, it's the best!"

That Kouplan recognizes this lightheartedness means that he'd once experienced it, too.

He thinks about Julia when he opens the browser. She's six and Liam is turning six. And although he's never met Julia, he realizes something: The energy is different. Julia is so quiet that even a librarian doesn't notice her. She goes to church and she sits at home and—what does she do at home? Watch TV? He scribbles his question in his note-book and keeps thinking. *Can you frighten a child into being constantly quiet?*

He looks for the address. At the apartment entrance where Chavez went in, twelve families are listed. Nine of them have typical Swedish *son* names. There's one *von* name; that sounds German. And there's a man called Morgan Björk. Kouplan's heart skips a beat. M.B.—perhaps common Swedish initials.

And one more name—a name right from Kouplan's childhood.

CHAPTER 26

That name had been on a class list, two names before his own, a million years ago. That's why he wakes up from dreams of social studies and reading—he's eight years old and the world's most competitive student—until he opens his eyes to find himself in a foreign country. A second later, fear as two eyes stare down at him. He screams and can't stop himself. His scream makes Liam start screaming, too. For a second, there's nothing but two screaming boys until Regina comes rushing into the room.

"Liam! You're not supposed to be in here! You know that!"

Kouplan calms his body down, the body that didn't know whether to fight or flee. *False alarm, dear body.*

Liam's lower lip is trembling. "But it's my birthday and everything!"

Regina strokes Liam's head and smiles apologetically at Kouplan. She explains to Liam that although it's his birthday, it doesn't change the rules about going into a tenant's bedroom.

"If you have a present for me, bring it to the kitchen table," Liam informs Kouplan and Regina laughs nervously.

"Kouplan doesn't need to give you a present. You'll be getting lots of presents anyway."

Kouplan lies immobile under the blanket as if chained there. If Liam, in his six-year-old enthusiasm had pulled off his blanket, he'd be half-naked. He keeps holding down the blanket as he says, "I'll be there soon."

He owns almost nothing. Three changes of clothes. One computer from the Stone Age. Two pens. One lighter. The money from Pernilla has gone to two months' rent, buying some meat, and setting aside for next month's transit card. Birthday presents had *not* been part of his budget. Nevertheless, he does have some money that can't buy anything.

At the breakfast table, he's invited to toast and soda pop.

"We *only* have soda pop when there's a birthday," Liam says as he eats a sandwich with bread still steaming hot from the toaster. His little sister is licking the butter from her toast.

Kouplan hands Liam his present. It's small and wrapped in a bag from the newspaper stand. While his bread is being toasted, he watches the child rip open the bag with such eagerness that his glass of soda pop almost gets knocked over. Liam's jaw drops.

"It's money!"

Regina leans over and looks at the coins.

"Wow, look, Iranian money!"

Liam holds them up, one at a time.

"That one is five hundred," Kouplan explains. "And that one is one hundred and so is that one. So it's seven hundred *rial* all together!"

Liam, now six years old and the proud possessor of seven hundred *rial*, can't sit still from excitement. *Julia would also be acting like that, instead of . . . of whatever she's doing. Whether she's been kidnapped or just picked up . . .* Kouplan thinks about what Pernilla has said about her memory. It almost seemed as if she's forgotten something extremely important.

Regina whispers as he walks past her to put his plate in the dishwasher.

"I hope you haven't given away too much money."

Kouplan smiles and shakes his head.

"Not enough to buy a pack of gum," he says.

Kouplan has been fitting fragments together in his mind. Julia being picked up by the authorities was one possibility. First, there's Pernilla's admitted memory lapse. Then, there's her choice of words when she said she'd felt that Julia was dead. That she had to let her go. So Social Services could have picked her up and Pernilla could have repressed the memory. It's a completely logical explanation, although you'd have to have a psychiatric illness to forget something like that. Kouplan's mother is a psychologist and Kouplan knows that such illnesses exist. And Pernilla, by her own admission, had been a patient at a mental hospital. She has scars from the cuttings on her arms and flight in her eyes. He could call Social Services, but they wouldn't tell him anything. They also have professional confidentiality about everything.

And then there's the theory about a father. *Who is the child's father?* It's been in his notebook for a long time and he still has no clear answer. Pernilla was angry when he first brought it up. When he asked about Thor, she'd laughed and said no. Then she had that look of flight in her eyes. Do her eyes always signal her need to flee?

Another theory deals with Pernilla herself. But it's a terrible one.

She calls just as he starts thinking this theory through, as if she can read his mind and wants to stop him.

"I couldn't sleep last night," she says.

"Why not?" Kouplan asks.

He realizes his question should rather consider whether anyone who lost a child could ever sleep again.

"I don't know if I'm paranoid, or . . . You know, everything is gone. I can show you the box where I had her lock of hair. Somebody's been in here and I'm lying awake afraid he'll come back."

"So are you afraid?"

"No, I hope he comes. I'll take him on. I lie awake and I'm ready for him."

Kouplan thinks about his horrible theory. Its draw-
back is if Pernilla herself were behind Julia's disappearance, why would she hire a detective to look for her? On
the other hand, it would make sense if she got rid of all
the evidence that Julia had actually existed.

"I can take a look at the box," he says. "Look for fingerprints."

Pernilla thinks it's a good idea. This speaks against his
horrible theory, but he decides not to drop it. His brother
often said: *Don't let go of your worst misgiving until you
have it all in black and white and with a key to Paradise.*

"That guy," Kouplan says. "The one you see when
you're out with your dog."

"Yes?" Pernilla asks as Kouplan tries to think how to
frame his question.

"What kind of a guy is he?"

"It's not him," Pernilla says immediately. "He would
never do anything like that."

"No, but what kind of a guy is he?"

"He's nice. Funny. We share a sense of humor. It really
can't be him. Once, it was raining and he held his umbrella
over me even though he got drenched himself."

"And he's never met Julia?"

"Not that they've ever talked to each other."

So, Kouplan thinks as he adds these bits of information, *Pernilla has met this man with his mutt many times.*

"So Julia was often home alone," he states.

"Just for short times," Pernilla says. "Twenty minutes

or so, when I walked the dog in the evening. Sometimes she was already asleep."

He hears her bad conscience. Twenty minutes out of twenty-four hours, when a single mom leaves her sleeping child alone. Her secret child, who was never allowed to talk to anyone. What do children do when they are not allowed to do anything? He gets an idea and also gives up one that said that Pernilla did not love her child.

"Was Julia able to read and write?"

He could have bitten his own tongue, but Pernilla doesn't notice he's using the past tense.

"Yes, fairly well. She can read some books all by herself. Why?"

"Does she know how to use your computer?"

"Not really. Well, she's watched me while I work. I do telephone support, but I use email, too."

"Could someone call you in the evenings?"

"In theory. But it's support for businesses. They call during the day."

"But let's say someone calls in the evening."

"Julia knows not to answer the phone."

Pernilla says this quickly, almost before Kouplan finishes his question.

Julia would never answer the phone, Kouplan thinks. *Just like Liam would never go into a tenant's room when he was sleeping. They're six-year-olds.*

"I can't stay at home," Pernilla says. "What can I do? Put me to work somewhere and tell me what to do."

•   •   •

Kouplan sends Pernilla back to Hökarängen. Chavez has never gone there while Kouplan has been shadowing him, and there's even the possibility that Chavez is the wrong man. There's the possibility that the person who took Julia goes on his merry way and an observant eye can find her.

"Stay near the subway or the grocery store," he says. "I can meet you there in a little while."

"I'm supposed to just sit around?"

Kouplan thinks about her memory.

"Keep on writing down more things you can remember."

"I've written a lot, almost five pages. I just don't know what I am supposed to remember."

Then there's silence on her end. It's quiet for so long that Kouplan checks his phone to make sure it's still on. Finally Pernilla says okay.

As soon as they've hung up, Kouplan remembers two more things and calls back.

"Can you check your phone for incoming calls during the past month?"

"Sure, I'll do it before I leave."

"And one more thing. When's Julia's birthday?"

"Her birthday?"

"Yes, what day was she born?"

"The . . . the third of August."

A reply that sounds more like a suggestion. So he asks again.

"August third, you said? August third, exactly?"

"Yes . . ."

Kouplan keeps silent. Sometimes she keeps on talking if he gives her time.

"Well, it was around the third of August," she says after a long pause. "Things were so chaotic back then. But we celebrated her birthday on August third."

Kouplan counts forty weeks back from August third six years ago. He thinks he should have asked if she could remember who called her then. He should have asked for access to her e-mail. What she can't remember might be digitally recorded there. He puts on the jacket that an angel had once sold him for just fifty crowns and glances out the window to check before he goes outside. He thinks about his classmate who had the same name as the family he is about to visit. Thinks about when he'd once been a completely different person.

CHAPTER 27

"That's what's hardest to remember." Pernilla gets caught on these words. They echo in her mind and scramble everything she's supposed to remember. She's written eight and a half pages of moments she's experienced, yet none of them can help Kouplan because he wants ones she can't remember. It's like searching for the back side of the universe.

He's asked her to think back to the time before Julia arrived and she understands that he really wants to know who she was sleeping with. But the only one was Patrick; she's absolutely sure of it. She digs deeper into her mind for anyone else, but if so, perhaps there were good reasons to forget. If anything else slips through, it's from an even earlier time. No, nobody else could have been Julia's father, even if there are months she cannot remember. Kouplan's like an employer who wants to know why there's a gap in her CV.

Hökarängen's subway station is practically empty.

While she waits for travelers to see if there's anyone she recognizes, she keeps writing. Every few minutes, she has a glimpse of a blond girl from the corner of her eye, but each time it's just a reflection from one of the windows.

I remember the arguments anyway. A child in the womb should not have to listen to arguments. It should only hear the shush of the body and Mozart. Patrick was furious over my choice to not let Social Services assume authority over Julia. According to him, I should be admitted to a psychiatric ward and Julia should be adopted or whatever. Since he was the father, you'd think he'd take over responsibility instead, if I were so mentally unstable. It takes two to create a child. The more I think back, the more I remember the arguments, the tone of his voice—even reaching falsetto—while everything I said just went past him. And there was so much crying. A child in the womb should not have to hear its mother cry. A mother is its entire world and if she's crying, it can't be good. I kept thinking about this, so I tried to be happy. Finally, I told Patrick to leave when I realized he was behind all the arguments.

Three people had come and now shared the bench with her. None of them are heading to the platform. She rereads her last paragraph; yes, she really was the one who'd told Patrick to get lost. It still doesn't excuse what he's done. He could have fought for them. A man in a black leather jacket is coming up the stairs. He's a big man and looks a little sullen. She keeps an eye on him through his reflection in the window. She's searching for a secret sign that he's the one who's kidnapped her daughter. She tries to feel that connection mothers have when their children are close by. But she's almost positive: Julia is not in Hökarängen.

Pelle Chavez is feeling irritated. It makes him do another round of bench pressing. He groans after this exertion and gets up from the bench. If they suspect him of anything, they should just ask. He's as pure as the driven snow. But a kid has followed him twice. He's just about 80 percent sure it was the same one both times. He knows the boss checks people out and he takes it as an insult.

The boy looks like the skinniest kid in the world. Probably not more than sixteen and looks like a stick figure. As he thinks about M.B.'s business, he imagines the kid is a direct import—an apprentice M.B. can break in or get rid of—who has no choice but to be loyal. If Pelle flicked him with his finger, the kid would fall down dead.

Questioning the boss would not be a good move, he thinks, as he lies back down for another set. On the other hand, he'd get points if he points the kid out to M.B. A sign that Pelle Chavez keeps his eyes open. Either that, or maybe he'll just beat the kid up the next time he sees him. He's bench-pressing two hundred and fifty pounds and concentrates on the bar, tensing his back, stomach, and chest. He decides to wait and see.

•   •   •

Kouplan smells a familiar aroma just inside the security door. He has to remind himself that the family with the Persian name could be kidnappers or criminals. They could be the people Chavez was visiting. He has to be careful. He takes a few deep breaths before he rings the doorbell. The door is unlocked and a wave of aroma hits him. No, you can't be a criminal if you can make such good *fesenjan*. A pair of questioning eyes looks at him. The eyes have the same color as his own.

"*Ba drood*," he says.

It's an educated guess. These names are totally Persian—otherwise he'd greet them with the Arabic *salaam*. The mouth under these eyes smiles and the scent of the chicken dish carries Kouplan away to other places.

"I'm looking for Nima," he says.

It's not really a lie. It's also the first time he's said his brother's name aloud in many years. The name echoes in his heart and he has to say what's on his mind at that moment:

"That smells absolutely wonderful."

The Sohrabi family consists of a mother, a father, and two daughters. The parents speak Persian with one another, but Swedish to the children, who'd probably been born here. The elder daughter is about fourteen, and the looks she's giving him make him uneasy. The chicken tastes like a bite of heaven.

"Nima," the mother says, looking at the father. "Do you know any Nima?"

Kouplan hurries to explain. "I just took a chance. I was searching on the web for people whose names he mentioned and you were one of them."

The Sohrabi family wants to know everything. When did Nima disappear? Were the police called in? Kouplan is lying about everything, and maybe they've even figured out he's lying, but they still ask him to write down Nima's name on a sheet of paper and they tell him they'll get in touch if they hear anything about him.

"Don't worry about it," he says. "I took you for someone else."

He waits for a pause in the conversation that would allow him to change the subject. Finally, he says: "You have a nice place here. I've always dreamed of living at Maria Square."

His true dream is to be able to live here without being scared to death. But the lies flow naturally, and why not be the guy he says that he is? He's already not the person he now is.

"Yes, we were looking between Maria Square and Medborgarplatsen," the father is saying. "Shaghayegh works here in Södermalm and I work in the city center."

Kouplan says that Maria Square was preferable, when you consider the location and the view. The elder daughter is pouting slightly and sticking out her chest in a way that makes Kouplan feel embarrassed.

"How are the neighbors?" asks Kouplan. He looks expectantly at the other members of the family.

The neighbors are polite and reserved and somewhat

impersonal for the most part, the parents both agree, but the daughter does not.

"Except for the ones upstairs!"

Shaghayegh's expression is difficult to interpret.

"Yes, one of the neighbors is a bit noisy."

"You could say that again," the daughter says. "Lots of people go in and out, too."

"Well, well," the father says with an intonation that the daughter ignores.

"You're the one always complaining!" the daughter exclaims. She's pleased by the attention. "It's hard to tell who's really living there!"

"So what name's on the door?" Kouplan asks, as if he didn't really care.

"We're allowed to talk to all the neighbors except them," the younger daughter explains. "Because they are bad people."

The mother and father look at each other. The father shrugs.

"Let's just say we'd never invite them in for *fesenjan*," he says. "But as for everyone else, it's not bad here."

"Well, they're the ones losing out," Kouplan says. "Because this is the best *fesenjan* I've ever had."

"Please have some more!"

"What's your name?" asks the younger daughter.

There's a moment of silence when everyone is thinking what to say without making anyone embarrassed.

"I'm sorry, I forgot to introduce myself," he says. "I'm Mehdi. So happy to meet all of you."

He feels like he's sitting with his own family. Almost. His own mother is perhaps not as good at making *fesenjan*, and nobody is discussing politics, but all in all it's almost like being in a time capsule of the world he's left behind. So it's not unreasonable that he's chosen to call himself Mehdi. That's his father's name.

He walks to the staircase, but pauses for a moment. Should he take a look at the apartment above? Or should he act like a normal person? Is the elder daughter of the Sohrabi family looking out the peephole at him? Probably. Does he really want to go upstairs and confront someone who is certainly a bad person, perhaps even a kidnapper? Probably not, but detectives can't always choose. Suddenly, the door to the apartment above slams shut and he shoots down the staircase and is out on the street before he can even complete the thought. He crosses the street as if he's in a hurry to get to the apothecary. He shuts the door behind him, surrounded by toothpaste and advertisements for medication. It's hard to see anything through the window, which is fogged up and mostly covered by advertisements, so he opens the door again slightly. On the other side of the street, a man is walking quickly away. Kouplan can only see him from the back, and the size of his nose is unclear. As the man turns the corner, he adjusts his pants.

CHAPTER 28

She doesn't dare say yuck.

You're not supposed to say yuck about food, no matter what, but not saying yuck is supposed to be a nice thing to do, not something you're terrified about. She eats her thousandth millionth cheeseburger. The first one had tasted good, but now cheeseburgers taste like disgusting men and being kept prisoner. When she looks through the window, it no longer even seems to lead to the air outside.

"Eat up, now," says the man who is not her father.

If he had been her father, she would say yuck. But this man is nothing more than one who steals children. He says that he's leaving for a week and she has to be a good girl.

"Tomorrow you will have a visitor," he says. "You're a big girl, now, you see."

She shakes her head. She knows she's not really a big girl. If he were her real father, he would say she's still a child. She can't imagine what will happen tomorrow, but she can tell by his voice that it's going to be hard.

"And then you have to do exactly what he tells you," the man says. "Otherwise, he will get angry. Did you see what Iwona looked like after a man got angry?"

She understands what he's telling her even if he's not spelling it out.

"It's important that you keep silent and do exactly what he wants," the man repeats. "I hope you understand me."

Then he goes out and locks the door behind him.

Then twenty-one red cars drive past on the street below. Other cars, too, but she only counts the red ones. Then it gets darker and it's harder to tell what colors the cars are.

Then it's night.

She still has the taste of cheeseburger in her mouth. She can't get rid of it.

Iwona is one of the grown-ups. One day her face was covered in blood and her cheek was deep purple. She didn't say a word about it. Now it's grayer. And a little green and a little blue. When Iwona saw she was staring at her cheek, her face twitched and then she tried to smile, but she couldn't.

She likes Iwona, even though she's only seen her three times. Of all the people in the apartment, Iwona is the only one she likes. She's now lying on the bed and counting all the people she hates on her fingers. The guy with the potato nose. The man with the accent. The man who says he's her father. And all the men who go into Iwona's room and make those sounds. They fill up all the fingers on her other hand and they are still there. Even though it's night. They're

groaning and banging and they're throwing around Iwona's furniture.

She can't understand why she'd just followed him like that.

She'd done exactly what her mother always said not
to do. It's just that she'd thought *those* men weren't real.
In her mind, they were monsters, drooling alcoholics with
staring eyes reaching slimy hands toward her. In reality,
it was a man in a normal jacket who'd winked at her and
asked her if she could help him.

Reality was a world where her mother was there every
day.

Lots of other things, too, which flutter in her mind like
photos from an album. Every day they seem less real.
Sometimes she's in the bathtub and asking her mother for
more bubbles. Her mother says there aren't any left, and
she's disappointed because she wants to make bubble animals. Then she wakes up and she's in this room.

She must be the dumbest kid on the planet. *Can you
help me,* that's all he had to say and she'd walked right into
his rough hands. One went around her waist and the other
over her mouth. She should have said: *I'm not allowed to
help strangers.* She repeats this sentence, the one she should
have said, in the dark. Practicing for the second chance she
won't have.

It's now silent in the room next to hers. The men have finished groaning and have left. She can't hear Iwona at all.
Not even her breathing. She's afraid. What if Iwona's dead?

In the dark, her thoughts become real. Iwona, white and stiff as a board, her heavily made-up eyes wide open with blood coming from them. Iwona dead on the other side of the wall and death crawling across the tiles, crawling to her room, crawling into her bed. Death wrapping around her like a blanket, no matter how hard she pulls it away. She feels her own throat is suffocating her; her own chest is exploding; death is whispering into her ear and through it: a cough. A dry cough on the other side of the wall. Probably not the cough of a ghost. As she listens carefully, she can tell that Iwona is breathing. They were just breathing at the same pace so it was hard to hear. She pulls her hand out from under the cocoon of a blanket she'd made for herself. Her knuckles knock on the wall. Three times. The room is so still as she waits as if time is standing still. Then there's a reply. Three Polish knocks.

Iwona is lying there, she thinks, as she turns over onto her stomach. She keeps thinking this over and over as Death slinks away into a corner of the room. You can do this with nightmares. You can drive them away by thinking of something else. Tomorrow she is supposed to get a visit. But maybe she will wake up and be in her own bed.

CHAPTER 29

In some dreams, you're falling and falling. Everything you try to hold on to dissolves and each time the hope of survival disappears even more. Finally, you wake up, but today Pernilla does not. She's sitting down as if paralyzed and she still feels as if she's falling and falling. She feels her mind fall apart into pieces and disappear as if it were nothing at all. The sofa she's sitting on feels as if it can't support her, perhaps does not even exist, and the floor is just as much an illusion. So she reaches for the one thing that still seems real, her phone, and she taps out a message that doesn't hold the slightest bit of her fear: *Could you come over for a while?*

Kouplan replies ten long minutes later: *Am leaving Maria Square right now.*

The fact that he will be visiting shortly makes her kitchen, her pantry, her stove, and her fridge become real. Even the inner chaos of her mind knows that the young man needs food, so she is needed and the fog in her mind must disappear. Behind her, the tapping nails and wagging tail remind her that another living being also needs her.

Kouplan thinks he'll ask: *Tell me about the man you meet when you're out walking Janus.* There's something about that man, about her walking with Janus, or, at the very least, how Pernilla talks about it that seems important. He thinks he'll say: *Tell me about the man you meet when you don't have Julia with you* but when she opens the door, her eyes are glassy and red and they focus on him the way a drunken driver tries to focus on a policeman. When she hugs him, she doesn't let go until he clears his throat in embarrassment. She doesn't smell like alcohol.

"Have you been taking something?" he asks.

"What do you mean?"

"I'm sorry I asked."

"I don't do drugs!"

Her voice turns angry and her face comes into focus. That's good. He'd rather have her angry than lost. They stand in the hallway looking at each other until she says:

"Would you like some cod?"

There's the Swedish mother, Kouplan thinks as he watches her whip two eggs into something the Swedes call egg sauce. *Then there's that naked soul which now seems to be dissolving. Her straight blond hair might as well be dyed rose with black roots; her light blue sweater might as well be a careless décolletage; the apartment might as well be a basement hole-in-the-wall.* He'd seen it before and he's seen it today and he felt it against his chest until she let go. She's like a person clutching at reality as if she needs it to survive. She's clutching it as if only her fingernails have a hold.

"Tell me about the man you meet when you're out walking Janus," he now asks.

He thinks she reacts, but it could also be his imagination.

"His name is Gustav," she says. "He has a mixed breed dog, too, one a bit bigger than Janus. And a female."

Kouplan nods and pretends he's watching her make the eggs. At least she knows the man's name.

"I believe there's a film called *The Dog Trick*," he says tentatively.

In reality, he knows the film very well. His brother had said: *When you're learning a language, watch movies and read books.* Kouplan remembers the line Alexander Skarsgård uses when he meets Josephine Bornebusch for the first time.

Pernilla wrinkles her forehead.

"You mean the one with Skarsgård in it?"

"Yeah, that's the one. Do you think Gustav is trying to get to know you better?"

"The trick of using your dog to meet girls?"

Pernilla smiles slightly, perhaps amused or perhaps pleased. The smile disappears immediately, but it had shown something about Pernilla and Gustav.

"Did he ever come here?"

Pernilla shakes her head, frightened.

"No, oh God, no! We just . . ."

"You just . . . ?"

He's responded too quickly. Pernilla shuts off and turns away. *What had they done and was it important?*

"I can understand why he likes you," he says, as relaxed as if he were not giving her a compliment. "You're pretty."

She glances at him with mistrust, so he opens his arms wide.

"Objectively speaking, it's true! I'm only saying it's not so strange!"

He sees her blush and thinks, *she's just lost a child.* He's only lost a brother, yet he knows that sometimes you need a break from all the sorrow and pain. Still he finds it odd that she's blushing. A part of him—and he doesn't want to know which part—also finds this interesting.

"We only went out for coffee," she says.

Fish with egg sauce turns out to taste like fish sticks: not much. Kouplan's stomach is still full of that heavenly *fesenjan* but he pounds down the cod and potatoes as if he's a chipmunk stuffing his cheeks.

In front of him is practical housewife Pernilla, but he'd just felt her fragility when she'd hugged him. The question was how deep her fragility went. The question was how difficult it would be to keep a child a secret when someone named Gustav wants to have coffee.

"Did you and Julia ever fight?"

"No." Her answer came quickly, followed by a sad smile.

"She was . . . always so positive and just . . . nice. She was born that way. I often thought that all the empathy people have lost landed up in her."

Not quite an answer the police would accept. Kouplan wasn't buying it, either.

"You must have had to say no sometimes. Kids get angry when they hear no."

Pernilla shook her head emphatically.

"Not Julia. She understood."

Kouplan thinks about certain regimes. Some of them say: *This never happens here* even as their prisons turn into cemeteries. He can't help the thought.

"Did you ever tell Gustav you had a child?"

If she says yes, it could be that she's throwing suspicion on him. If she says no, does she realize that she's throwing suspicion on herself? She wrinkles her forehead, looks at him.

"I don't believe I did."

How can a person be a mother and not even mention her child? Kouplan has three ideas: One is fear of being dumped. One is the habit of not telling anyone. One is the pretense that the child does not exist.

"So what did you talk about?"

"Mostly his business."

Kouplan can't make sense of this. Perhaps he should dig into why she didn't tell Gustav about Julia. Ask a direct question. But direct questions haven't worked yet. It's as if they close her down and extinguish her eyes.

So he doesn't say anything and keeps on eating cod

with egg sauce. Pernilla has put down her silverware. She's sitting quietly but finally she finds something to say.

"He wants to start a business making apple jelly."

Kouplan's notebook has dog-eared pages and a bent cover. Notes are randomly distributed with arrows pointing every which way. They're in Persian, Swedish, and even some English. He knows where everything is and the patterns they're making.

"What have you written there?" Pernilla asks.

"The description of the various people Chavez has met."

"And there?"

"What you can see from the Maria Square apothecary."

It's not what's really written down, but he has no intention of letting Pernilla know she's one of the suspects. That would just make her sad. She points to another word and he laughs.

"That's in Swedish," he says.

"But what's it say?"

"Bead mosaic kit," he says. "Obviously."

"No, it doesn't."

When she reads the word, he realizes that his spelling is not at all what the word had sounded like to him. But he really hadn't had time to ask her how to spell it.

"I don't even know what it is," he says.

She gets up and goes to her bedroom. She comes back with some various bead mosaic pictures in happy colors.

"You put beads on this backing and then when you
have a finished pattern, you iron them and they melt together. This one Julia made."

Most of the bead mosaics are pink, violet, red, and
blue.

"Her favorite colors? They're very pretty."

Often when you talk about a six-year-old's creativity,
you have to be diplomatic. But these bead mosaics are
actually quite good. Symmetric and with excellent patterns.

"Did you help her?"

"I just taught her how. These she did all by herself."

"Wow."

He notices his *wow* fills her with pride and touches
her heart. Tears appear in the corners of her eyes. *It's pretty
crazy to suspect her*, he thinks. *She's the one who hired me,
after all.*

"I have more, but . . ."

Her voice starts to tremble and he doesn't need to see
more.

"So what have you written down?" he asks instead.

Pernilla has written eight and a half pages. Tight, hand-
written, and with the years in the margins.

"I tried using the computer," she said. "It went better
when I wrote by hand. I don't know if you can read my
writing."

Kouplan can read it. Pernilla's hand is like that of a
child. The letters lean in every direction, but her printing
is the finest he's seen. On the first page he reads: *The rain*

was so strange the day they took Julia. When he flips to the second and third pages, he can see the dates skip around: earlier years, different months, back and forth to days where Julia learned how to walk, learned how to crawl. Anecdotes and soul-searching.

"I'll take this home and read it thoroughly," he says.

"Thanks."

"Not to worry."

"No, I mean it." Pernilla looks right at him and nothing in her face is hidden. "Thank you so much for . . ."

When she takes his hand, it warms everything in his blood, rushing through his body with the message of touch. He wonders if she realizes this. When she looks into his eyes, he has to remind himself to look at her and they haven't even been drinking any wine.

"I'm not sure that you're really twenty-eight," she says. "You look like you're twelve. And yet you're wise like a hundred-year-old."

It's gotten dark, so maybe she doesn't see that his blood has finally reached his face. He laughs to dismiss his blush.

"There's a Persian saying," he tells her. "Don't be fooled by the size of a peppercorn. It may be small, but it is strong."

"Say it in Persian."

This embarrasses him, too, in spite of the fact that he's supposed to be as wise as someone who's one hundred years old.

"Felfel nabin ce rize, beškan besin ce tize."

She smiles and her eyes look like they must have been when she was having coffee with Gustav.

"Falafel bise rise, beska nissekisse."

Compared to her pronunciation of Persian, his spelling of bead mosaic kit is nothing at all.

CHAPTER 30

The house with its wooden fence and iron gate is dark as coal inside, except for a corner of the reading room, where a floor lamp shines down on an armchair, a round table, and Thor. On the table are collections of photographs in green envelopes. On Thor's lap is a photo album that he'd labeled *Sofia*, from his time as a priest at that church. He has group photographs of Sankta Lucia parties, weddings, and baptisms and now he's peering through his reading glasses at a photo in his hand. He could have already been sitting there for ten minutes. It's hard to feel time passing when it's dark outside. The photo is one of a church coffee hour and the reason for the picture was the violinist, who is elegantly dressed and in the middle of playing, his bow raised. It must have been a special occasion. Thor doesn't remember what it was, although he does remember the blond woman sitting on the right. She's at the very edge of the picture, so it appears as if her cheek is elongated, but still it's impossible not to recognize her: Pernilla.

Very strange that a boy named . . . Cupcake? . . . that this young man would come here to his home and ask questions about Pernilla. Thor rarely has a bad conscience about his profession's need for confidentiality—like life itself, he cannot choose—but just this once it might have been helpful to be more forthcoming. Just three words would have sent the boy away with the answer he was looking for, but there's a reason for the practice. He cares for souls; if Cupcake had wanted his soul cared for, he'd have done so, too. But it's not right to reveal one soul's secret to another. He sends a wordless prayer to God, but, as usual, God is a bit too distantly divine to give him an immediate answer.

He looks at Pernilla's elongated cheek for another moment and strokes it with his thumb. He wishes he could have done more for her. Perhaps she didn't really need a priest, but still she'd come to him. There are some lambs that the shepherds remember very well. Even shepherds who are retired.

He slides the photo back into its slot in the album, where it resembles all the others. No one else would see the complicated life behind an elongated cheek on the right; just himself and the few people Pernilla feels she can trust. He hopes that Cupcake can do something with the words he'd sent him away with. Unfortunately, Thor feels he didn't choose them very well.

It's dark in the small room for rent on Hallonbergen. Or just "the room" if one would ask the Swedish Welfare

Services—the ones who decide who gets housing sub-
sidies. This room, as dark as it is, has been rented in
secret. Just one lamp shines at the head of Kouplan's bed.
It's shining on eight and a half hand-written pages and
Kouplan blinks so he can focus his sleepy eyes. He's decided to write ten relevant questions about this material
before he goes to sleep. So far, he's only come up with
three.

He decides to order things chronologically and then
reads Julia's life story from being a one-year-old to be-
coming a big girl, almost school age. At the end of the
episode where Pernilla and Julia had gone to Skansen,
Pernilla had written: *If you're a six-year-old child, you get
into Skansen for free. Next summer, she'd have needed a
ticket.* His eyes ache, but he keeps them open as he focuses on the sentence: *Next summer she'd have needed a
ticket.* Are those just words, or did Pernilla not want Julia
to grow older?

He presses his eyes shut and then opens them again.
Writes a rather odd question, because he still has quite a
few to go to reach ten.

4. Was P afraid of J growing up?

When he reads the question again, he realizes it's not
so odd after all. If Julia was not registered, what was she
going to do when all the other kids started school?

Julia learns to walk over the kitchen floor. Julia stops
using a pacifier. Julia meets a swan and Pernilla is scared

to death—the first thing she thinks is that someone has taken Julia. Who?

5. *Who was P protecting J from, and why was P afraid?*

A relevant question.

Julia and Pernilla go to Skansen and sit on the large Dala horses. They're talking about fathers and Julia almost manages to pet a squirrel. Julia says her first words. Pernilla and Julia paint watercolors. Julia shows a natural talent for color. At least, according to her mother. They borrow books from the library. Julia wants a dog and on her sixth birthday, they get Janus. Julia gives Janus his name.

6. *Did Julia only meet animals and never any other people?*

7. *How tall are the Dala horses?*

8. *Are the paintings still around?*

He's writing these questions randomly, because his lack of sleep the past few days won't let his pupils focus. But this *Ten Questions on the Text* technique he'd learned from his brother and it is a good one; sometimes it works on your subconscious. You just write down all the questions that come to mind, no matter how easy or inconsequential they seem. And after eight and a half pages, one more question appears:

9. *Was J never angry?*

He has difficulty believing this. The only children who

are never angry are those who are undernourished or in deep depressions. Pernilla must have suppressed all memories of an angry Julia. Perhaps those memories would lead them to the answer. Instead of thinking of a tenth question, he sends a text to Pernilla: *Keep writing!*

Kouplan brushes his teeth and his tired eyes ache.

Thor brushes his teeth and gargles with mouthwash.

When Kouplan spits, he thinks about Pernilla's light blue bathroom.

When Thor spits, he thinks of caring for a soul and what it means to be a priest.

Kouplan thinks about the child's toothbrush in Pernilla's bathroom.

Thor thinks about the moment he finally completely understood what Pernilla was saying to him.

Kouplan already imagines the relief his body will feel as soon as it knows it will be allowed to fall asleep. He sets his alarm clock so that he won't sleep for days and he crawls under his blanket full of love for his wooden bed frame and foam rubber mattress.

Thor checks the front door and looks out at the dark November night for a few minutes. He has done what he could, he thinks, as he walks back to his bedroom. He's listened to a soul—one that had been difficult to understand. He crawls beneath his down comforter and believes that God forgives those who try their best to do the right thing.

They turn off their lights at the same time.

CHAPTER 31

It's time to research Morgan Björk. Kouplan gets off at Maria Square along with hundreds of other people. At least half of them must be police officers, but at eight in the morning, they're too busy rubbing sleep out of their eyes, like everyone else, while clutching their warm coffee cups.

Morgan Björk. Maybe it's just an unfortunate coincidence that this man has the same initials. Maybe he has nothing to do with Julia, Chavez, or selling women. Kouplan is not sure whether Morgan Björk lives on the top floor where the Sohrabi family identified "bad people." But in his notebook, he has *the boss, the bad people,* and *Chavez visits* all in the same place.

On the other hand, maybe nothing of this entire story makes sense.

One thing he has no intention of doing is to ring the doorbell. Not the top floor apartment and not anywhere else in the building. He has no intention of standing outside and waiting and no intention of entering either the drug store or the art gallery.

As he turns into that street, he realizes that he has no idea what he's going to do. He only knows what he's not going to do. A man in a beret and a woolen jacket comes walking toward him. He can't just stand here. The man in the beret could be one of M.B.'s henchmen, one of his business partners or some kind of customer. Perhaps he put on this beret so he would look as little like a criminal as possible. He could also be a border policeman. *Think quickly, Kouplan, think in a millisecond!* He chooses the apothecary and pulls at the door without result. Tries again. The man in the beret glances at him, informing him in a dry voice:

"They don't open until nine."

The man opens the entrance door to the apartment building next door to the apothecary.

Kouplan slips in behind him before the door shuts.

There's no scent of *fesenjan* in the stairwell of the beret man's apartment building, but Kouplan can smell lemon-scented cleaning liquid and the stone staircase. On the ground floor, the apartments belong to *Larsdotter* and *Kleve*. Kouplan walks up to the second floor and shivers when he thinks that police officers could be living in this very building, so close to the police station. He tries to look like an average citizen and thinks he should be carrying a bundle of newspapers instead of Pernilla's eight and a half pages. Nobody is ever suspicious of a newspaper delivery boy heading up the stairs. There's no sound from Larsdotter or Kleve. They're not opening their doors and they might well be already at work.

On the fourth floor, Kouplan finds a window. It's small, rectangular, and facing the street. He wonders what you call this kind of window in Swedish. Every single corner has been cleaned.

On the other side of the street, the sun is finally reaching the roof of the apartment building where the Sohrabis live. Nobody is moving behind the windows. He thinks of their daughter and a smile tugs at the corner of his mouth. She's going to be a handful, he thinks. He wonders about the kinds of trouble he must have caused his parents at that age. He dismisses the thought as quickly as he can.

Behind another window, there appears the body of a young man shaking in a strange way, but after a few seconds, Kouplan realizes that this man is practicing a dance by Michael Jackson.

The apartment directly above that one has blue striped curtains and blinds. There's a gap of a few inches. Yellow light shines from behind them. And there's a head. He squints to sharpen his view; yes, that's not a flowerpot. Kouplan's heart begins an irregular beat and he's breathless, but not from climbing the stairs. There's a small head behind the windowsill and beneath the curtains, a face with an empty gaze looking at the street.

Look at me, Kouplan prays with his entire soul. He peers to see her better; it's her, isn't it? *Look at me!* Even if it's a taller person sitting down, he's pretty sure this isn't an adult but a child's face. An adult would not be staring out the window like that.

Kouplan tries to attract the child by waving his arms behind this rectangular window, although he realizes there might not be enough contrast from the other side of the street. He uses Pernilla's papers. They'd be white against the background. He puts them against the window-dowpane, white on black, and pulls them up and down until she catches sight of them. There's the width of a whole street between them, but he can tell the exact moment her gaze is caught by the dance of the paper. He hurries to put his face against the window, waves so as not to lose her attention. *Julia?*

There's a man waving to her from the building across the street. He has dark hair and he might be dangerous, but he's really thin. It's the first time anyone has waved at her, especially from the house across the street. She's afraid if she blinks, he'll disappear. He's making signs with his hands. He's pulling up and down, as with a rope. Finally, she understands what he means. Without losing his gaze, she pulls at the blinds—they first go down and then they go up. He gives her a thumbs-up and smiles and he doesn't look dangerous at all . . . even if she now knows that looks aren't everything. *We're like two angels,* she thinks. *Two angels across from each other, high above the other people.* She can see him take a picture with his phone. Deep inside, she knows he's not with the other men.

•   •   •

How can you send a signal across a street to a six-year-old through two windows? He could write on the window or on a piece of poster board if he had one, and she could nod or shake her head. Pernilla had told him that Julia knows how to read. But he doesn't have a marker or any poster board and even if he did, the letters would have to be enormous for her to read them. That's why he decides to take out his phone. If Julia can't say who she is, maybe Pernilla can. He takes two pictures. The first one is extremely blurry and the second one less so. He chooses the one more focused and pulls up Pernilla's number. He wishes he could be at her side when she gets it, and then he clicks send.

Is this Julia? Pernilla reads the message many times and feels her pulse increase. She was on the toilet when the phone vibrated in her pants pocket and she doesn't move for five minutes. The picture is terrible, but she still thinks she recognizes Julia. Her hair seems brown, though, but that may be due to the darkness in the room. The face . . . at first, she's absolutely sure it's not Julia; then she's sure it is. She closes her eyes as she holds the phone with trembling hands. She opens her eyes and recognizes her child. And then she doesn't.

It takes an eternity before he gets a reply from Pernilla. A timeless eternity on the third floor, with the sound of movement from an apartment below and a dust-free window nook made of stone. Out on the street, the sun has finally reached the windows of the uppermost apartments. A woman in a woolen coat is walking past on the street below. A man in a red jacket is entering a building. When his phone finally buzzes, it's not the answer he was waiting for. Pernilla asks: *Can you take another picture?* But he can't. Someone has closed the curtains of the child's room.

CHAPTER 32

Someone has left a half a cup of coffee at the back table in Fåtöljen Café. Whenever one of the employees walks past, he sips from it as if he were a paying customer. The coffee is cold, but it still gives him energy.

He takes out his folder with Pernilla's eight and a half pages. He's decided to read through them again in the light of day.

Can you take another picture? Is that a true reaction from a mother who sees her child? He takes out his phone and looks at the picture again to determine how blurry it really is. You can tell it's a child, but he has to admit that his Ericsson T610 hardly measures its picture quality in megapixels. He opens the folder.

The rain was so strange the day they took Julia. Tiny drops, a heavy mist almost, but slowly and imperceptibly, you still got soaking wet. Julia noticed it, too:

"Look at the rain, Mamma! It's not really falling.

It's like those tiny mosquitos, what are they called, Mamma?"

She turned her face up to me, her tiny nose damp, and her hood fell off her head for the fifteenth time in a row.

Kouplan tries to see the child in the apartment as the one who is turning up her face with a wet nose. The face on his phone is somewhat in shadow and rather thin. His logical side tells him that you can't tell from anyone's writing if you've taken a picture of the right child. At least, he can't tell from Pernilla's writing.

There is one large and one enormous Dala horse at the center of Skansen. When we went to Skansen, Julia and I, she was not impressed by the bears or the moose, but always wanted to go to the Dala horses. We'd go there starting in March. I'd bring cheese sandwiches and we'd climb onto their broad wooden backs. They gave us a sense of security with the log cabins around us and then the whole fence surrounding all of Skansen itself. We were sitting on the enormous horse with Julia and me carrying on a conversation.

"There's a daddy," Julia said.

We looked at the daddy walking past pushing a baby carriage.

"Yes, there's one," I said. "Look over there—there's another one."

From our positions on the enormous horse, we watched daddies go past.

"I don't have a daddy," Julia said.

I remember the taste of cheese and bread crumbling in my saliva. With one hand, I held onto Julia and with the other, I unscrewed the top of the Thermos.

He has trouble making sense of this text. It's probably that Pernilla's faded memory messes up her text, but were they each sitting on one of the horses or were they both sitting on the same horse? *Their wide wooden backs.* He'd searched for those horses online and he now knows just how enormous they are. Surely a three-year-old would not be sitting alone on one? Probably not, since Julia was holding on to her with one hand. And she's unscrewing the top of the Thermos with the other. And eating a sandwich. All at the same time. Five feet above the ground.

Her description of Skansen reminds him that memories can be unreliable. They're modified truths, which makes Pernilla's entire production a precarious basis for his analysis. He'd once talked about this subject with his mother. There were studies about unreliable witnesses, she'd read, and she taught him that his memory could deceive him. *But you can also see the gaps, and the jumps in memory tell as much about the truth as correct memories. It all depends on the truth you're really looking for.* Those were the kinds of things she'd talked to him about, as if he would understand them even though he was still young.

I still can see her enraptured face, her light freckles, the way she couldn't take her eyes from Janus. Even though the dog was still called Challe then. But on the way home, you could see the change in him, how his posture straightened and how calm his curly coat became. He left the shelter as Challe, an ownerless mixed-breed dog, but he got off the bus as Janus, the dog belonging to the Svensson family.

"Why Janus?" I asked as we rode up the elevator.

Julia grimaced in the way she had, as she does when she's trying to pull something over on you. She peers through one eye and pulls in her mouth; something is going on inside her original, very own mind.

"Because we were in a shelter and Jesus took shelter in a manger, but we can't really call him Jesus, can we?"

It's the only time Pernilla mentions freckles. Probably because they adopted Janus in August and the sun had had time to speckle their faces. Julia was able to enjoy her dog for two months. The dog that was to give them a sense of security.

The motivation for giving the dog that name is odd. It's weird enough that a child thinks that Janus sounds like Jesus and even weirder that a child connects the concepts of a doghouse and the manger Jesus was laid in. But Janus is the name of a completely different god, one that would be unlikely to appear in Julia's thoughts. Kouplan is better at his Persian mythology than his Greek and Roman ones, so he notes down *Google Janus.*

"Can I take this for you?" asks the waitress as she gestures at the cup and saucer next to Kouplan's papers.

Do you know anything about Greek mythology? Kouplan wants to ask her. That would be more like the real Kouplan, if he accurately remembers who he'd been before. But asking that would make him easier to remember. He nods as anonymously as he can and says, "Sure, that's fine." His stomach growls.

Before he leaves Maria Square, he takes another walk by the house. He breathes deeply as two police cars drive past him just inches away as he looks up at the window with its curtains drawn. If he didn't have the photo, he'd wonder if he'd really seen anyone up there.

Without Pernilla's corroboration, he can't just storm into the apartment on the top floor. The child could be a completely normal child, about to have breakfast with her family, reaching for some toast, and then there'd be a phone call to the police. There are children in every apartment building in this city.

Plus, people who are involved in criminal activity are very observant, to say the least. What if he appears in the building for a third time, going up the same stairs past the Sohrabis and Björk's apartment? And if M.B. himself is using his apartment for criminal activity?

The door to the stone staircase across the street is shut. He doesn't even look up. He walks past the building like any person at all walking past and he's thinking that Pernilla ought to recognize her own child and whether or not it really was Julia in the picture. And there's one more thing that comes to mind: Julia's shoes.

CHAPTER 33

The girl stares at the man's red jacket. He hung it on the chair when he came in, but it's upside down so the arms are dangling toward the floor. He was just suddenly there, her visitor, and his hands were big and as angry as hungry wolves. Fear is screaming in her ears: *be nice.*

CHAPTER 34

He's thinking of the shoes the whole way home. His mind makes connections via the gaps and patches of memory: repairing clothing, shoes wearing out. He realizes he's thinking two different thoughts about those shoes: they'd have to be either completely new or fairly old. He's going to check this when he gets home.

He puts rice to boil on Regina's stove and then walks over to the children's shoes and inspects them. Liam's are small and Ida's are even smaller. Liam has dark green rubber boots and Ida's are red with pink roses. Kid sizes thirteen and eight and a half. The lock over Kouplan's head rattles and he's so frightened he starts to cough. Regina opens the door and stares at him. Kouplan blushes and keeps coughing as he drops Liam's boot as if it were his secret lover.

"I was just checking the size," he says once he's able to speak.

"Okay, but may I come in?"

Kouplan would like nothing more than to go hide in his room, but his rice isn't finished yet. And Regina is looking at him with such amusement that he has to say something.

"What size shoes would a kid have at six?"

"That's what you want to know?"

She laughs and he feels himself blush again. This is not really his thing.

"Well, no, but . . . can a six-year-old wear size eight and a half?"

"Probably, but it would have to be a tiny six-year-old."

That's it. Julia was supposed to look almost seven.

He wonders what he's really trying to find out. It would be easier if he were looking for a specific lie, but all he has is things not fitting properly. Not just the shoes. Also the jacket.

Once he gets to his room, he Googles the Roman god Janus. His search comes up with: *Janus opens and shuts the portals of heaven and is therefore shown as having two faces: One that looks backward in time and one that looks forward.* The picture shown does not really look like Pernilla's fluffy mutt. But it does resemble a sculpture decorating a hallway in upper Sundbyberg.

And the bathroom, he thinks. In Regina's bathroom, there are all kinds of things: nose drops and bandages and thermometers and thousands of tissues. Plus a changing

table. In Pernilla's bathroom, there is just one pacifier and
one big and one little toothbrush. Both brand new.

He would love to ask his mother some questions.

His suspicion is one he ought to reject, because he's being
paid to believe Pernilla, but as he thinks about it, he realizes he can find no objections. He thinks about bead mosaic kits, Thor, photos, kitchen chairs, and what happened
six years ago. He needs a shower, but his thoughts don't
even give him ten minutes to rest. Before he goes out of
the apartment, he goes into the kitchen to Regina.

"I have a weird question," he says.

Regina looks at him. It's probably the first time he's
talked to her twice in one day.

"Shoot!" she says.

"If you give birth, is there a lot of blood?"

"Yes, that and amniotic fluid. Why do you ask?"

He doesn't reply, so she asks, "You haven't gotten anyone pregnant, have you?"

The question warms his heart, just the idea that he
could get someone pregnant. But he doesn't answer. Instead he asks:

"And the embro . . . umbril . . . the cord thing?"

"The umbilical cord."

"Yes. Is it thick or thin?"

Regina laughs.

"I know, it's a weird question," Kouplan says and tries
to laugh himself.

"Well, it's about this thick." She shows him by measuring the space between her thumb and her forefinger. "Thicker than a finger, but not by much."

"How do you get rid of it?"

Regina wrinkles her forehead.

"I mean, what are you supposed to do with it?"

He laughs again, hoping he sounds disarming.

"That is, I'm not planning on having a kid. I just have to know. My friend is pregnant and she has all kinds of questions."

"Well, you cut it with scissors."

"Like those?" He points to Ida's pair of kid scissors. They have red polka dots.

Regina smiles. "Obviously, they have to cut through thicker things than paper. It's a heavy pair of scissors. Sometimes you have to cut the cord a few times before it separates. The cord is pretty tough."

"I thought it was soft?"

"It's tougher than it looks. More like an octopus arm than a pair of pantyhose, if you will allow me the expression."

"Okay. Thanks."

"Is that it?"

"Yes."

"Your friend doesn't want to know if it hurts?"

He shakes his head, because he has to get going. He has to go to Pernilla's place and look with new eyes.

"She already knows it hurts like hell. Thanks again!"

• • •

When Pernilla opens the door to her place, he looks into her eyes as if he can read an answer in an iris and a pupil.

"Maybe it's Julia," she says. "It's just so blurry."

"You mean the photo."

"Yes, but I think it's her!"

Kouplan is studying the hallway, just like he did the first time, but now he's not looking for what's there, but what isn't.

"Aren't we going to go get her? Where is she?"

"Wait a minute."

Julia's jacket is still hanging at the same spot as before. It still looks brand new. The shoes (size seven and a half) have no signs of wear.

"I just need to check Julia's bed."

He walks ahead of her, through the kitchen in the apartment, which is something other than he perhaps believed. At Regina's place, there's a child safety catch on the oven. Not here at Pernilla's. On a hook, there's a red-and-white child's apron.

"Do you wash things often?" he asks as he bends over Julia's bed.

The sheets have My Little Pony on them. They haven't been washed much.

"Every other Sunday. Why? I usually don't run into anyone when I go to the laundry room, if that's what you're . . ."

"May I look at Julia's clothes?"

"They're in the dresser."

He pulls her clothes out of the dresser and puts them

on the bed. Julia has twenty tops, all bright pink, a few pairs of pants, no underwear, five T-shirts, and three pairs of socks size 33–35. Kouplan feels his heart pumping information to his brain. The walls seem to undulate. Pernilla, astonished, watches him.

"What are you doing?"

Maybe he doesn't know her at all.

"Do you have any drawings she's made?"

Pernilla goes to get a folder.

"I've kept most of them," she says. She opens it. "I even bought one of those plaster sets, you know, the kind where you can make imprints of hands and feet."

The pictures are simple. Flowers, houses, squid, and octopi. The lines are perfect. Not a single brush has been pressed too hard against the paper. Nothing falls outside the lines.

"Do you still have the plaster cast of her feet?"

He's amazed how normal his voice sounds.

"No, something was wrong with the plaster. It was too runny. Kouplan, talk to me. What are you looking for?"

He closes the folder with its perfect flowers and perfect houses. He takes some deep breaths. He needs the oxygen.

"Pernilla."

"Yes?"

"Can you tell me about giving birth to Julia?"

Kouplan's acting very odd.

"It's important," he says. "Please."

Pernilla doesn't want to think about when Julia was

born. First, because it was a day filled with fear. Second, because nobody was with her. She'd even called Patrick, but he'd hung up on her. *I can't deal with you*, he'd said. *I'm giving birth!* she'd screamed back. All he replied was: *Don't ever call me again*. Kouplan's velvet eyes are looking at her. She sighs.

"It was a very difficult day."

All she knew was her time had come. She couldn't call anyone. She had the emergency number on her phone just in case anything went wrong. She was determined that Social Services was not going to take her child, but she also did not want to die.

"I lay on the floor." She pointed. "Over there."

She doesn't remember how long it took. Maybe several hours. Maybe fifteen minutes. She remembers sweating. She remembers how her body hurt like a fleshy extension of her fear. And then.

"But then when she was here . . ." she says. "When she was here—a tiny human that was all mine. It was worth it."

Kouplan is watching her, though barely meeting her gaze.

"And then what did you do?"

"Held her. Dried her off. Felt extremely relieved that I didn't die."

"What did you do with the umbilical cord?"

Pernilla is still feeling her relief: The fear had turned to a memory because she was alive and she had Julia.

"The best thing that ever happened to me," she emphasized truthfully.

"The umbilical cord, Pernilla. Did you cut it yourself?"

She nods.

"Which scissors did you use?"

"I don't remember. I only have two pairs. One for the kitchen and one for paper."

She doesn't understand what he wants from her. Maybe they can find some clues in Julia's bedroom. Fingerprints of the person who stole Julia's lock of hair. Maybe now Julia's drawings had also disappeared. She'd have to check the folder again once he was gone. But what does she have in her memory about an umbilical cord?

"Could you . . . I know this sounds strange . . . but could you lie down and show me how you cut it?"

"On the floor?"

"Preferably."

Pernilla lies down on the kitchen floor. She puts a towel beneath her rear, as she'd done six years ago. For a second, she feels an old feeling: *This is not my body*. It sweeps through her like a spirit.

"I was lying here like this."

"Did you catch her with your hands?"

She nods, because she's suddenly not so sure.

"I think I got on my elbows like this. So she wouldn't hit the floor."

"And the umbilical cord?"

He handed her the kitchen scissors. She shows how she cut it—halfway between where Julia was lying on her chest and her lower body where Julia had just come out.

"So it was fairly easy."

"To cut it, yes. Giving birth was hard. It was terrifying."

"Was the cord soft?"

She stretches her legs, looks at the ceiling. Tries to remember, because it must be important.

"Yes, it was like, like an intestine . . . giving what a child needs. You can think of a long balloon. But not blown up."

"As easy to cut as a pair of pantyhose?"

Lying on the floor is more emotional than she'd expected. It was an echo of what she had experienced that day. She remembers how the walls seemed to storm.

"Approximately."

Even if you can't see everything behind an iris and a pupil, Kouplan can tell that Pernilla is not lying. She's stretched out straight on the floor, a blond woman of about thirty, and she's speaking from her heart. But there's the truth, and then there's modified truth. Julia's twenty tops are as fresh as if they came right from the factory. Julia does not own a single pair of underwear. And there's no parent in the world who does laundry only twice a month.

He often feels that he needs his brother. But today, he really needs his mother. He calls forth her face, with her glasses and her brown locks that have just started to go gray. Mama: First, is it possible? Second: What's the question? His picture of her does not say anything, but he knows what she would say. First, everything is possible with the human psyche. Second: The answer comes to the one who does not question her experience.

"Did anyone ever accuse you of not being pregnant?"

He can see her answer both in her iris and in her pupil. Her blue eyes seem to hang on to him and they alternate between truth and modification.

"Everyone did."

CHAPTER 35

At first, she was just one of many church visitors. During the service, she sat in a pew far back. She recited the Apostles' Creed, but did not come up for communion. She looked like she'd come to the wrong place . . . something about her body language.

After the service, he thought she'd gone home. But during coffee hour, she turned up. She picked up a small slice of sugar cake and sat at an empty table.

"She seems lonely," Hasse, the organist, said.

"I'll go talk to her," Thor said.

Her smile was forced and shy. She held out her hand.

"I'm Pernilla."

"I'm Thor. Are you new to the congregation?"

Her eyes almost met his, but got lost. Her nervousness might flow into him if he didn't sit down, so he did.

"We haven't been to church for a long time," she said. "But I needed some peace. It's been so . . ."

She was quiet for so long that he thought she wouldn't say anything else. But a good shepherd knows how to listen.

". . . stressful," Pernilla finished with a sigh.

Her sigh let him understand that she wasn't talking about the stress of catching the bus every morning.

"Do you have anyone to talk to?"

The question triggered something.

"I refuse to go to a psychologist!"

That day, Thor handed her a brochure concerning conversations about the care of souls.

The next day, she called and made an appointment.

All kinds of people come with the need to speak about their souls. People in mourning, people who were addicted, people who were rejected or filled with guilt. During the first ten minutes, Thor tried to put Pernilla into some category in order to understand what she needed, but she seemed to hide from his scrutiny and skittered away from him. Finally, he leaned back to let the Holy Spirit enter the room. That was when she began to relax.

"I feel so confused," she says. "Perhaps it shows?"

Thor let the Holy Spirit fill the room.

"I believe you are afraid."

And Thor believed it. Pernilla reminded him of other women who needed more than just spiritual help. She was picking at one of her bracelets.

"I don't dare tell you."

"I will keep what you say in professional confidence,"

Thor said. "You need not be afraid of what I might say to other people. What you tell me in this room, I cannot repeat to anyone else."

"You can't report things?"

He shook his head. "Not even criminal activity. My professional silence is complete."

This seemed to calm Pernilla.

"I'm afraid Social Services will find her," Pernilla said. "I can't stop thinking about it."

He hummed as if he understood.

"Who are you afraid they will find?"

Pernilla nodded toward the floor.

"Julia, my daughter."

It seemed she thought Julia was in the room with them. Did he miss seeing a child enter the room? Nobody was hiding behind Pernilla. Her nod could be a tic.

"How old is Julia?"

"Three. Julia, say hello to the nice priest. It's all right."

No three-year-old appeared from behind the chairs. Pernilla smiled as if she wanted to excuse her daughter's behavior.

"She's so shy."

Caring for someone's soul means listening and understanding. One has to be careful with the souls of human beings.

"I believe I'm at fault for her being so shy," Pernilla said. "I feel such guilt sometimes . . . but I really don't want to lose her."

Pernilla started to tell him a fantastic story while Thor

was trying to see into her true soul. How they'd threatened to take her unborn child. How she faked a miscarriage and decided to have the child at home. How she now had given birth to a child who was not registered—she gestured toward the floor again. He could have said, "There's no child there." But he did not want to lose her thin thread of trust.

"Why were they threatening to take her from you?" he asked instead.

"I was in the psych ward," she explained. "Because I tried to commit suicide. But that was before Julia came."

"You mean Julia helps you to feel better."

Pernilla smiled.

"She gave me something to live for. When you have a child . . . it's like you're able to see the light again. The light she sees."

"That sounds wonderful," Thor said.

He meant it. Whether or not this child existed, it seemed wonderful for Pernilla's broken soul.

"I'm just . . . I'm thinking all the time that they're just going to come and take her. It makes me so afraid."

There are priests who believe in demons and there are priests who believe in modern psychology. Thor believes more in the latter than the former, but Pernilla's statements about psychologists during the church coffee hour told him that she was not receptive to that. And if they gave her medicine that took away the only thing that made her happy, what would that do for her soul?

"Could it be," he asked. "Could it be that you are

worrying yourself unnecessarily? Social Services usually doesn't come around for children they don't know exist."

Pernilla was silent for a moment. She glanced at the floor and then back at him, looking him right in the eyes.

"That's what I thought. But it sounds so much better coming from you."

That was their first conversation regarding the care of her soul. As Pernilla got ready to leave, she leaned over and seemed to pick up the weight of a child from empty air. She mumbled something toward her shoulder.

"Aren't you going to say good-bye? Say good-bye to the nice priest."

Thor did not know if he was making the right choice. All he knew was that Pernilla was feeling much better than when she'd arrived and he knew he had had to make a choice. He reached to the invisible being next to Pernilla's cheek and stroked it.

CHAPTER 36

Kouplan asks Pernilla to sit down and he's going to lie to her. As she sits on the sofa, he says, "Pernilla, I'm going to tell you what I believe and you have to decide if I'm telling you the truth." Then he starts to lie.

"I've been thinking about a few things. Like Julia's shoes in the hallway. When was Julia wearing them?"

It's the worst kind of interrogation even though it's Kouplan, with his velvet eyes, who is asking her. This is not making anything any better. Her body gets goose bumps from worry.

"She has shoes, she wears shoes, what's the matter? Shouldn't you be out looking for her?"

He's supposed to be out looking for Julia. He's not supposed to be making her feel uncomfortable. Her legs and arms feel like they're falling asleep. Isn't she paying him to look for Julia?

"It doesn't make sense," Kouplan explains. "She should

have a much larger size, perhaps size seven and a half especially if she's tall for a six-year-old."

It's creeping, creeping, creeping and Pernilla has to close her eyes to hold back a headache in order to answer, as if she needs a veil between herself and the world.

"So what? Maybe my daughter has small feet! I doubt very much having small feet is a crime! I'm not a criminal for having a daughter with small feet! Should I be arrested because my daughter has size seven and a half?"

She's just talking as she often does if she's under this kind of interrogation. Maybe they are behind him? Maybe they sent him?

"Of course, she may have small feet," Kouplan says soothingly. "Let's talk about something else. When was the last time you bought Julia a toothbrush?"

"I don't know."

"Was it recently?"

"I don't know. No, no, no—it wasn't recently. Are you now a dentist, too?"

She doesn't want to be so mean to Kouplan, but he's pressing her. It's that veil—she loves it and he's trying to rip it away. It's sky blue and covers her memories. There's blood and sorrow behind it.

"It's brand new," Kouplan says. "We can go look at it, if you'd like. It's never been used."

Pernilla is torn by everything she has to feel. The veil she must keep in place, the fear someone has been in her apartment and took Julia's toothbrush. Maybe Kouplan did it.

"And her clothes," he adds. "We can go and look at them if you'd like. They're also completely new. Some still have price tags on them. And there's no underwear."

She doesn't know why that last sentence hangs in her mind. Maybe because it is so direct and yet so normal. Kouplan is looking at her, a question in his eyes, and she wants to attack him and say, *Of course she has underwear* but she can't remember if she's actually bought any. And if there's no underwear, well, you have to wash pants more often and she doesn't remember washing Julia's pants at all.

"You do the laundry every other week," Kouplan says, as if he's following her thoughts, "but kids get clothes dirty really fast. Even calm, quiet children. She has only three pairs of socks. And, Pernilla, her jacket has never been outdoors."

Don't say it! The words scream in Pernilla's mind.

"And those drawings you said she made. Not even a great artistic talent can draw like that at the age of three. And, finally, there's . . ."

Don't say it!

"When a person gives birth, the umbilical cord is not as easy to cut as you said. I've talked to a mother and you can talk to her, too, if you'd like."

How does she know that Kouplan is not one of them? That that woman who had a child is not one of them? That they haven't been sent by the mental hospital to trick her? In her mind, she is trying to find the most logical explanation. She has an idea of what he wants to do. He wants to tear down her entire world and kill her child.

"I pay you to believe me," she says, but it comes out as a whisper.

"And to help you," Kouplan replies. "Nobody is going to a basement storage room to steal three photos from the hard drive of an old computer. Plaster does harden around a foot, if there is a foot for it to harden around."

It's as if his words are coming out like blood. She wants to wipe them away and cover them over, but they're tearing at her beneath her skin. *Don't say it!* Her breathing is quick and shallow and she's pushing the air out before it has time to enter. She's deciding whether or not to trust Kouplan. What he says is logical. Someone from Social Services would definitely know what a bead mosaic kit is. She takes a deep breath, even though she's struggling with herself: *Don't tell me!*

"Tell me."

His lie is incredible. His lie is so true that it kills her child.

"Get out of my house!" she exclaims.

She points a shaking finger at the door.

"Think for a minute," he says. He's coaxing her with his eyes.

Pernilla doesn't want to think about it. She wants Julia back, even if Julia's clothes never need to be washed. Even if Julia has small feet and talks like an adult. Her eyes sting, tears run down, snot . . .

"You're lying," she says.

Because if he's not lying . . . she can't breathe, she

keeps struggling to breathe, her head spins. If he's not lying . . .

"Thor has met her," she says.

Kouplan looks at the clock. Hesitates before he says, "Why don't we give Thor a call?"

In some magic way, he has Thor's number.

CHAPTER 37

"Thor Lejon."

"Hello . . ."

"Hello, this is Thor Lejon."

". . ."

"Hello. I don't know who's calling, but it is one thirty in the morning."

". . . it's Pernilla."

"Pernilla? How are you, Pernilla?"

"Hi, Thor."

"How are you doing, dear child? What's on your heart?"

"Things are crazy here."

"Has something happened?"

"I have a question. Just one question . . . okay?"

"Of course. But what's wrong? Has something happened? A young man came to visit me the other day and asked about you . . . what's your question?"

"Julia. You know, my daughter."

"Yes."

"This is an odd question, but . . ."

"You can ask me."

"It might sound crazy."

"Maybe it will be hard to understand?"

"It's sick, actually. But you know that I was in the psych ward a long time ago."

"I remember you mentioned it."

"But as I said, this is an odd question . . . a really strange question. Okay?"

"Okay."

"It might be the craziest question you've ever heard."

"Pernilla, I care about you, you know that. But it's one thirty in the morning and I would appreciate it if you would just ask me your question."

"Okay. Sorry."

"God will be with you."

"Okay."

"And your question?"

"You know, my daughter Julia. I'm wondering . . . I'm wondering . . . does she really exist? Is she real? Kouplan just told me she doesn't . . . Hello?"

"I'm still here. If Julia exists . . . she lives in your mind and in your heart, Pernilla."

"I know. But does she exist outside of my mind and my heart? Is she real?"

"Well, then . . . Then I'd have to tell you, no. No, she doesn't exist in reality."

"Are you absolutely sure?"

"Yes."

"Damn, hell, shit, fuck."

"Would you like to talk about it?"

"No."

Click.

CHAPTER 38

Kouplan wakes up on Pernilla's sofa again. Julia has been gone for two weeks and three days. He'll have to go to Maria Square before they move the girl to another location. He should shadow Gustav and shouldn't limit himself to Hökarängen. He sits up before yesterday's events catch up. Then he thinks, there is no child, and then, once again, more slowly:

There is no child.

He really ought to take a shower. Still, inside him, his mind is churning. How can there not be a child? His entire notebook is filled with clues! The ticket agent at Globen. He opens his notebook and looks between the lines. He tries to recreate the conversation. The ticket agent had seen a man with a child. On a Monday, right? Did he say what time? No, just that he went to McDonald's and ate a burger.

The girl at the subway booth. When was she working? Did she even see the same man the ticket agent had seen?

How could it be so exceptional to see men going on the subway stations with their daughters? Kouplan stares at his clues: just people who had seen people.

Except for the librarian. She remembered Pernilla from the photo and remembered her daughter. Somewhat, at any rate. Only after Kouplan had described her and pointed out she was a calm, quiet child. But with hesitation.

Everything else was a hunt for Chavez. The guy who runs errands for another man who, according to Kouplan's fellow landsman's landlord's friends, runs business with women and children and doesn't seem to be connected in the least with Pernilla or Globen. Spending the night on a staircase in Akalla, observation from Vita Hill while needing to pee, risky sneaking around Maria Square. Kouplan rubs his overheated forehead. He's probably a complete idiot.

Pernilla has slept for ten hours. She has to check the clock again when she wakes up. Is it really eleven thirty *in the morning?* Then everything hits her. The serious conversation with Kouplan the night before; it wasn't a dream. He had lifted her from the floor and, with determination in his velvet brown eyes, asked her to sit on the sofa. He'd said, "Pernilla, I'm going to tell you what I believe and you have to decide if I'm telling you the truth." She'd steeled herself against him, knowing that he was going to lift the lid on everything inside her. And it would hurt.

Julia is gone, much more than she could ever have believed.

Which has to be impossible, because she still can remember her scent and her mild smile. The little body growing year by year. It's impossible that that body had never existed.

But it never had. Kouplan had demonstrated it for her. They looked at Julia's toothbrush together. He was right—it had never been used. Julia's clothes—unused. She'd been so cute in that top with the ladybugs—now, she'd never worn it at all.

It's a shadow of a morning that turns into the shadow of a day. If you can call all this disorientation a day. Sometimes, she thinks she doesn't exist, either. Not to mention Kouplan.

"Maybe you are the illusion," she says, but she doesn't have the energy to give emphasis to her statement. "I've only known you for a little while. Who can say that you are more real than my child, whom I've known for six years?"

He doesn't argue. He just asks:

"An illusion that came to ask why your child hasn't needed any new shoes since she was four?"

She shrugs. Glares at the boy who says he's twenty-eight and who could just as well not be real. She could blink, open her eyes and he'd be gone. She looks at her own hands. They might as well be empty air.

"What is reality?" she asks.

Kouplan nods. "That's a philosophical question."

"If I know someone, do I really know them?"

"I think the problem is that everything happens inside our heads. Even we . . . who've never had non-existent children . . . build our thoughts on a reality that we think we see and hear and feel. And if we don't really hear or see or feel, maybe it doesn't exist, at least to our minds."

She's a human being, too. One who hears, feels, exists.

"And the opposite is true," she says.

"Yes, the opposite is true. But then we start to compare our realities with each other in order to figure out what the world is really like."

A moment of silence is broken by a thud. Pernilla stares at Kouplan, who stares back.

"If we both heard that, then it's real," she says.

"I think it's the mail."

He's holding the phone list from the phone company. He decides to throw it out without looking at it. Nobody needs to know who may have called when Pernilla was away and Julia was alone at home. He's finished—*case closed*—and he should go home.

"Why do you think she disappeared?" he asks instead.

Pernilla slowly shakes her head. She looks like someone who's just gotten shocking news about reality.

"I don't even know why she was born."

"Were you pregnant?"

"Yes."

He decides not to ask anything more, because it's not the kind of thing people like to talk about. But she leans forward, looks directly at him.

"It's true about Social Services. They did want to take her as soon as she was born. Because I was mentally unstable."

She says this as if she's reading from her medical record.

"It's sick that they have such power over other people's lives. How could they know what kind of mother I would be?"

Kouplan has no idea what kind of mother a person who dreams up the life of another person might be. But Pernilla gave him a half a chicken sub sandwich and nobody else has ever done that.

"I think you'd be a fine mother," he says.

"So, when I had the miscarriage . . ." she says, and then falls silent.

Her eyes search the room, trying to fasten onto reality.

"Well, at the time . . . I couldn't grasp what had happened. But at the same time, I was pleased because then they couldn't come and take her."

Kouplan can't imagine being pregnant, having a miscarriage, or being institutionalized in a psych ward, but he does his best.

"Maybe your mind reordered everything," he says. "You kept what felt good and got rid of what made you sad. The miscarriage."

Pernilla makes a humming sound as if she's agreeing with him. She leans her head back and stares beyond her white ceiling.

"Everything was all mixed up."

She doesn't need to say anything else. *The psyche is fragile*, his mother had once said. *The psyche is fragile and the world is hard*. But Kouplan is still wondering why Julia disappeared.

"Was she getting older, just like a normal child? Has it been more than six years since she was born?"

"Yes."

Pernilla thinks some more.

"Well, she talked early, she spoke in a mature way. She was wise beyond her years. But you're talking about the years going by."

"How were you going to work things out when it was time for her to go to school?"

"I was thinking of home-schooling her. But that would be difficult when she got to the upper grades. I thought about all that a great deal, because I can't . . . you know, timetables and all that."

Different parts of her mind are reconnecting, Kouplan realizes. He wonders what new connections are forming, especially in a person who could invent an entirely new human being from scratch, and explain away the lack of this person's photographs or why the plaster cast of her foot didn't take. Still, it is entirely logical to worry about what a child needs to learn in the upper grades. His mother would have been fascinated to meet someone like Pernilla. She wouldn't find it at all unpleasant.

"Julia would no longer be a small child," he says. "Perhaps, with her age, it was starting to feel difficult. Your brain couldn't deal with it anymore."

Instead of answering, Pernilla hits herself on the side of her head. It's so sudden that Kouplan leaps up to save her from herself.

"I don't understand my own mind," she says. "I don't get it! What's going on in there? Did I ever tell you I used to hear voices when I was a teenager?"

"No, you didn't."

"People told me that those voices weren't real and I came to understand they were right. I never saw anybody, but the voices kept saying the weirdest things."

"Such as?"

"Oh, they babbled. Like: *Uncle Lalala at the edge of nothing and lalala and Uncle has no wool, macaroni and more, you know.* You must think I'm crazy."

According to the normal definition of the word, it fit Pernilla.

"The psyche is fragile," Kouplan says. "And the world is hard."

"It's a good thing I knew I heard voices, or I would never have believed you."

"You didn't believe Patrick."

She shakes her head as if Patrick isn't part of the discussion.

"I was pregnant, of course."

Kouplan wonders if she ever had an inkling that Julia was not real, especially since she'd become aware that the voices from her teenage years were never real.

"Did you ever think about the fact that you never washed her clothes?"

"No. But you don't always think about routine things. Now that you think about it, though, it is really odd, isn't it . . . you have to look at it in a whole new way."

Kouplan notices that she says *you* instead of *I*. Perhaps she doesn't want to take it too personally.

"You miss a lot," he agrees.

People miss things. There's that experiment where some young people were asked to watch a movie of some kids playing basketball in black shirts and white shirts and the test takers asked them to keep count of how many times the ones in the white shirts had the ball. After watching the movie, they were asked if they'd seen anything unusual. Most of them had not noticed that there was a person in a gorilla costume walking among the basketball players. He'd even stopped and thumped his chest. They were much too focused on counting the times the white shirts got the ball. Kouplan had read it somewhere and put it into his memory. Not to relate to psychotic victims of crimes who weren't crime victims, but to always stay alert, to always be aware of border police.

It's a shadow of a day and with every breath: *Julia does not exist*.

Pernilla has perfect eyesight, but she knows what astigmatism means. Nothing can focus. No matter how much you try, the picture is never sharp.

She understands this feeling so well.

CHAPTER 39

The room is now her entire world. The walls, the ceiling, the window that only leads to empty air. She's nine years old and she ought to be in school. They were supposed to be learning the names of the lakes.

She's writing a list of five things in her head. Not one that she'd be doing in school, such as an essay about *My Favorite Candy* or *The Best Songs*. This list is *The Worst Things*. She has enough time to weigh each choice and re-arrange the list, because sometimes she thinks one thing is worse and sometimes she thinks another thing is worse.

Number Five. That George calls himself my real father and lies about my mother.

He thinks she ought to say "Hello, father" when he walks into the room. Ever since she overheard his name, she says "Hello, George." It irritates him and she really ought to be smarter than trying to rile up her kidnapper, but it's the only resistance she can give. Yesterday he came

in after the disgusting man had left. He told her that
her mother had moved. In her joy at being free from her
troublesome daughter, her mother had moved to Russia
to follow her dream of being an actress. She did not ask:
So, then, what did she do with my siblings? She also did not
tell him how much her mother hated Russia. She keeps
her memories tightly to herself. It's information George
does not have. She's not stupid.

Number Four. That I didn't scream.

She's really stupid, in fact, because she didn't scream.
Sometimes, her mother comes to her in her dreams. She
hugs her with all her warmth, but sometimes she opens
her jacket with the zipper and it's black as night in there.
She speaks the worst words: *I'm so disappointed in you.*

They were supposed to learn the names of the lakes
and on Friday they were going to have a geography test.
Maybe Friday is already over. She would have studied with
Laura. Laura would cover Rāza on the map and she would
have guessed right. She already knows a number of the
names of the lakes. That's why she was looking forward
to the test. Mamma, Tētis, and Erki would often go fishing with her before the new baby came. After that, she'd
fish with Pappa and Erki. She wonders if they are fishing
right now. This very second. If she'd just done one little,
little thing, maybe she'd be asking to go fishing with them.
If only she'd just opened her mouth and yelled as loud as
she could. She closes her eyes and pretends she's far away
from here.

• • •

Number Three. That that man did some really disgusting things.

She closes her eyes so hard it almost hurts, but it's not enough not to see. Because his hands were on her skin and skin is like a huge eye that never forgets. He had a disgusting tongue, disgusting nails, and a smile like a normal man, which made it extra disgusting. But none of that was the worst.

Number Two. That George called this "the first time."

The worst was George coming in long afterward, smiling and saying she'd done well for it being "the first time." She understood what he meant: This had just begun. She was supposed to be happier next time, the man had told George to tell her. But for the most part it went well. It will be easier and easier each time, but she had to remember to smile and be happy. Think of something fun, he'd said. Think of candy.

Number One. That I'm in a foreign country and nobody knows.

Her legs feel like they could run the whole way home to Mamma and Pappa. But she knows it's just a feeling, because the car driving her here took an eternity. The space she'd sat in had no windows, but she could feel the difference in the jolts and bumps on the roads. Sometimes it was quiet around them and at other times she could hear noises and voices. She could have screamed then, too.

Being in a foreign country is a loneliness as great as the darkness of the night. Laura, Mamma, Pappa, Erki, and the baby are in their normal world and she's in a foreign one. All she has left is her own arms and legs. She hugs them and scratches them, because this disgusting man has covered them with his smell. Where her feet end is where the foreign country begins. Maybe it will swallow her up.

She'd realized she was in another country ever since she realized she'd spelled A-P-O-T-E-K. In her country, an apothecary is spelled A-P-T-I-E-K-A. There's no "o" in it.

CHAPTER 40

Janus scoots between the living room and the hallway with a determined and ever increasing desperate look at Pernilla. She sighs. "He'll pee on the rug soon," she says. "Do you want to walk with me?"

A simple walk hasn't been part of Kouplan's world for the past two and a half years. It's crazy to be outside when he doesn't need to be. He's thirsty for real air.

"Only if I can hold the leash," he says.

A person with a dog on the leash is a real citizen.

She decides to take the long walk. The November air is starting to be real winter air with a chill that burns the cheeks and gives the day an aura of reality. Frost glitters in the trees.

He pulls on the leash, because Janus has stopped to smell some poop. Pernilla glances at him. The boy who has his own problems and still is able to understand her.

"Do you like dogs?"

He makes a face that could be a yes or a no.

"Right now, I love them," he says. "Janus makes me look normal."

She thinks they have a great deal in common. Of all the people in this city, perhaps she's the one who understands him best.

"Sometimes I let Julia stay home so nobody could see her."

"More and more often, I know," he says. "But you said it was because she was getting tired of Janus."

"It was a bit of both."

Janus trots along with his short legs. Pernilla can watch him better now that someone else is holding his leash. He sniffs a gold spot in the frost, and then sniffs the air. He's finding a tree interesting.

"I wonder if he feels what we feel," she says. "Did you know that a third of a dog's brain is connected to its sense of smell?"

Janus stops and turns his head. Then he's pulled from his trance by a tug on the leash. Then he starts to sniff a leaf. Pernilla has to smile.

"I really like that dog," she says.

Kouplan watches the busy bit of life attached to the end of a leash. A living being, totally dependent on Pernilla. How does it feel compared to the needs of an imaginary child? Did she start to notice the difference between having a real dog on her lap and having a child made up of empty air? Everything originates in the mind, even the sensation of

heat and cold on the skin. And all the background pro-
grams running along in the subconscious; they keep our
routines going as if our brains were a bunch of old com-
puters.

"Patrick had a statue in the hallway," he says. "Do you
remember it?"

Pernilla wrinkles her forehead as she searches her
memory.

"It was the one with two faces," he says.

She nods at once.

"Yes, we had that at home," she says. "It was this Greek
god, as I remember. I'd almost forgotten it."

"Roman mythology," Kouplan says, and then hopes
she forgets he was trying to correct her. "He represents
beginnings and ends."

"I know. One face looks to the past and one face looks
to the future."

"In your writings, you said that Julia picked the name
Janus because it reminded her of Jesus."

Pernilla nods as she looks at him.

"Yes, she did."

"But if Julia was in your mind . . ."

Her eyes narrow.

"I mean, the Greek god," he chooses to use her termi-
nology. "His name was Janus, right?"

Janus the god can handle being confused for a Greek.

"He's given his name to January, the first month," he
continues. "The god of . . . doors and bridges . . . new
beginnings . . . transitions."

"Transformations," Pernilla says.

She stops. "How weird that Julia chose that name."

She doesn't need to hear again that Julia was all in her mind.

"A good choice," he says.

If his mother had been around, he'd ask her what she would think of his theory. That the dog had triggered Pernilla's mind to start to find its way out of her psychosis. There are various schools concerning psychological illnesses. His mother is one who searches for triggers and reasons in the labyrinth of life. He watches the wriggling, tail-wagging mutt on the leash and wonders whether a dog would help him miss her less.

"Are you certain that they're looking for you?"

"What do you mean?"

"You're so scared all the time. Are you sure it's not your imagination?"

Kouplan no longer has the letter that told him to get ready for deportation. He did not want anyone to know who he really was, so he intended to burn the letter. He doesn't really remember if he's followed through. Still, he can't get at the file they have on him at Immigration Services. In a way, Pernilla's question is relevant: She couldn't prove that Julia existed, and so Julia does not exist. He has no proof that he is allowed to exist.

"I wish," he says. "If I woke up and everything was shown to be just paranoia . . ."

He tries to imagine this. First, that the police he's

always trying to hide from are imaginary. Second, that he'd wake up from a psychosis. The relief that would feel like is something he can't imagine.

"I'd cry," he says.

Pernilla glances over at him. It would be a real coincidence if one mentally ill person trusted another mentally ill person to search for a child that was just imaginary. She knows crazy people attract other crazy people, so she'd brought up the question. But deep down she knows that Kouplan has something she lacks. Balance.

"I'm sorry I had you running around all over the city," she says. "You shouldn't even be out on a walk and I had you running back and forth between Globen, Akalla, Hökarängen . . ."

"And Maria Square," he says. "No need to apologize. It was my job. I just wasn't looking in the right place."

"But I feel really bad about it now," she says. "I should have . . . I even understood somehow . . . remember when I was crying and saying I thought Julia was dead? And if I'd been following my feelings, I might have . . ."

Kouplan is no longer listening, so she stops speaking. He's picking up his phone and pulls out a photo, shows her, even though Pernilla's already seen it.

"Do you think she looks kidnapped to you?"

The child looks like a normal girl. It's what she thought the first time she looked at the photo. *How could I tell if it were Julia if she looks so normal?*

"I thought you said Julia didn't exist," she says. "So nobody could kidnap her if she's not real, right?"

"I'm not so sure."

Kouplan does not know. Julia may not exist, but Rashid exists. Rashid's landlord exists. Some of his sympathetic friends know that a man named M.B. trades in women and at least one girl. Chavez exists and when he left the building in which the Sohrabi family lives, he said he'd been visiting *the boss*. Many people had been going up and down the staircase and the Sohrabi daughter says that there are bad people there. And in that apartment, there's the face of a young girl. It's a clue beyond Globen and a pink raincoat.

"I don't know," he says.

There's a scale. On one side, there are people who throw themselves in front of cars to save the life of a kitten or give away everything they own to starving people so they have food. On the other side, there are psychopaths who kill for an earring or sell out their people for the sake of oil. Somewhere in the middle are most people, and Kouplan is one of them. He may be a good listener, but he's just an average good person. He will definitely not risk his life calling the police for a child who may—emphasis on *may*—be held captive in an apartment on Maria Square. When he thinks this, he thinks that this doesn't sound like an average good person, so he doesn't want to think it again.

Janus has now sniffed several hundred leaves, pine-cones, and piles of poop. He trots into the elevator ahead of Kouplan and Pernilla.

"Theoretically," he says, because he can't shake the echo of his thought about the girl, "if you want to call the police, but you don't want them to trace the number . . ."

Pernilla thinks about this. The elevator goes from one to two.

"If I call a customer, all they see is the support number," she says. "But the police can trace it, I'm sure. Why do you want to call the police?"

"Something I'm thinking about," Kouplan says.

CHAPTER 41

The world has two sides: winners and losers. One side has people who are used up, consumed, thrown out. The other side contains those who see where the cards are going to fall and want to land on the winning side. George is in the middle of such a game and his advantage is that he can see this clearly. He sees the losers before they even know they've lost. He can't see all of M.B.'s tentacles, but he knows they exist. He feels that he, himself, doesn't have any, so he pretends they're not there. He's a decent guy who's figured out how the world works.

For instance, he'd never have sex with the little girl. They asked him to, but he refused. Sex is between a man and a woman. That pervs exist who would pay huge amounts of money to do so brings up the question of their morality, not his. You hunt or are hunted—that's how it is—but you can choose a few of your own rules.

For instance, he's not making himself into a boyfriend; that's an extremely effective method. He agrees with M.B.

about this. Katarzyna, for example, she's in the psychological gap between love and hate right now. Each time he
says, *how are you, baby,* he confuses her even more. Women
are weak like that, as fate would have it. It's funny, they
even call it the Stockholm syndrome. *Don't you love me?*
he asks and goes nuts every time she says *no,* even though
he's an average guy. He decides to have gentle sex with her
when she says *yes,* and rough sex when she says *no.* He's
the strong one.

But a seven-year-old without tits? *That's my limit,* he
thinks. *Sex with a fifteen-year-old, maybe even a fourteen-
year-old. A thirteen-year-old only if she's well developed with
big tits and an ass that asks for it.* He can feel an erection
building up, but it's at the thought of those big tits, not at
the thought of a thirteen-year-old. He's going to make a
sandwich and then go in to Katarzyna and ask her if she
loves him. Or Iwona, because her breasts are fuller and
juicy. Even if she's M.B.'s "girlfriend," this is one of the
perks of the job. Even better than a free pass for the gym, he
thinks, smiling. Puts his teeth into his ham sandwich and
that makes him think of hams, Katarzyna's and Iwona's
and the fictional thirteen-year-old's.

The point is, he's an okay guy. When he got the call
to find a child under the age of eight, it was obvious that
he'd be the father and not the boyfriend. He wasn't sure
what M.B. was thinking there, but finally M.B. agreed. The
concept of *your real father* is going to work. It's a proven
method.

It was ridiculously easy to lure her over to him. Almost

as if it were her fate. As he usually thinks: The market feeds the demand and the world runs a strange system. He's just a cog in the machine. He does what's needed and doesn't make mistakes. He even made sure he had a Y chromosome when he was born.

The eagerness in his pants has subsided a bit—he can think about making another sandwich before he goes in to Iwona. Katarzyna is going to get a customer soon, too, and he has to watch the door. He makes his second sandwich as a classic ham and cheese.

Y chromosome, he thinks, and is amused by his own train of thought. It was like winning the lottery. The world has two sides, and if you're born a girl, it's pretty much a given that you're going to be consumed and go under. Perhaps they even like it, but he is still glad he was born a man. He wonders if this insight makes him a feminist.

They're going to change apartments soon. M.B. is looking for a new place and then he'll move the business. Either a suburb or in the city, but it has to be close to people's jobs and preferably not so close to the police station. He wonders if he should tell Katarzyna about the move. It would bring her closer to him, if she felt he were telling her a secret. He's got a crumb on his chin and he's about to brush it off when all hell breaks loose.

Laima sees them come. They're getting out of a van like the one they brought her in, but they've parked around the corner so she can see only the back of the van. They're tumbling out like huge gorillas and they are lining up

along the wall so that she has to press her nose to the window to see them all. Somehow she knows they're after her
and her heart is racing like a train—if a man could do
something as bad as that disgusting man, how much would
ten gorillas do? Her eyes fly around the room. There's no-
where to hide, not even a closet. Just the file cabinet. But
even if she could throw everything out—papers and
boxes—there's still not room for her legs in one empty
drawer. She runs to the window again and the men in
black are gone from view. She decides: *If they come for me,
I'll jump.*

The building thunders as they break in. It sounds like
hundreds of men's voices all yelling at the same time. The
lock on her door seems as sturdy as paper. All her courage disappears. She can't jump, because then she'll die. So
she goes underneath the bed and presses against the wall.
The door opens. Big, black shoes are thumping and stop
right in front of her. She does not dare to look, but when
she shuts her eyes, it gets even worse. Hundreds of black
arms could be reaching for her and she wouldn't know.
She opens them again and sees the face of a man upside-
down. He's smiling but his eyes are wild and he's calling
in a foreign language to someone else. Her heart bangs
against her chest.

But no black arms reach for her. The face goes away and
now someone else is sitting on the other side of the room.
He is talking to her in a foreign language, but she doesn't
say anything. His voice is kind, but so was George's. After

a while, he leaves. Laima shifts position, because she can't just lie there for all eternity. There's lots of dust and brownish gray dirt.

The next person to come into the room is a woman. She takes off her jacket and lies down on the floor by the other wall. She waves to Laima. "Russki?" she asks. Laima doesn't reply. "Polski?" Laima keeps her mouth firmly shut.

You can't trust women, either. There was a nice woman in the first apartment named Jessica. At first you could think she was nice, but then she went crazy and was threatening everyone with a kitchen scissors. Both men and women could seem nice and then turn into monsters. That's what these past weeks have taught her about human beings.

But then Iwona comes in the room. She sits beside the other woman on the floor and she bends over so she can see Laima. Then she knocks, three times, on the floor, just like she does at night.

Laima has to decide if she can trust anyone. If she can't she'll remain, all alone, in a foreign country—a nine-year-old beneath a bed without money, food, or parents.

"Latvia," Iwona says to the other woman. Her voice sounds like someone who also had visits during the day and also had been locked into her room at night.

Laima takes a deep breath, gets dust in her nose and almost sneezes. The bed has wooden slats beneath it, unfinished and with splinters. She knocks on them, three times.

CHAPTER 42

Kouplan isn't there any longer. He'd left Pernilla's apartment two days ago. She could almost think that she'd imagined him. She called him once, just to check, and he reassured her that he really exists. But perhaps a convincing hallucination would also have done so.

No matter how crazy she is, she has decided two things. The first one is that Julia had existed.

"Thank you, my dearest," she says to the empty air.

The thing was, Pernilla should have died six years ago. It was going to be pills and she would have made sure that whoever found her was warned ahead of time. You don't want your death to be too traumatic for the living.

She was so lonely after Jörgen died. It was a loneliness that turned her inside out. You'd think it would dissipate with time, but the only thing that changed was how people's sympathy waned. It's customary to grieve for one year, not longer.

Patrick looked like a duplicate of Jörgen. His posture, the features of his face—as if he were a carbon copy. He answered her anxiety and released passion with kindness and encouraging exclamations. Jörgen wouldn't have been encouraging—he would have loved and laughed with a brutal self-confidence. He would have laid his tattooed hand on her naked breasts and felt her heart.

She and Patrick had been together for eight months before she understood how mistaken she had been. They'd just moved in together. Most of the moving boxes were gone and their home was an orgy of good taste and middle-class dreams. Not a single book in the wrong place. Not a single unpaid bill. She realized that her loneliness was as acute as ever. It was as if her heart were being squeezed in the five fingers of a hand, squeezed harder day by day. One more inch, and the marrow in her bones would grow cold. Another inch. Patrick thought she was "getting pale" and told her she ought to find a hobby.

At first, she felt nothing only once in a while. Then it came more often. Finally, it was constant. She could feel nothing but emptiness and the emptiness gripped her harder and harder. She found the words *self-harming behavior* wrong, because when the razor cut, it loosened the grip of loneliness and pulled warmth out with her blood. Only her arm hurt, not her being.

She had been so desperate to get rid of her anxiety that she's still not 100 percent sure. Even though she's assured Kouplan that Patrick was the father. Still, Patrick was the one who'd called her parents and told them she'd been committed. He actually called her fucking parents. *How inconsiderate!* she'd yelled at him. He didn't understand what he'd done. He told her that it was not necessary to scream at him like that.

Seeing her parents added another feeling in the mix. Not just that cold loneliness but also overwhelming nausea. Finally, Patrick had an explanation why she was vomiting all the time; the hospital had her tested and she was pregnant. But Pernilla knew the whole time that her nausea was not caused by Julia.

She had already been planning suicide when the blood came. That is, she'd already planned how to do it so that it would be easier for everyone. Of course, she couldn't kill herself as long as there was another life inside her womb, but it helped her to think about it. As soon as Social Services took her child, then she would do it. She had the pills; she knew what she was going to write in the letter. And when she saw the blood flowing from her, she knew it was time.

It's just that there was a glimmer of life left in her womb. A glimmer of life that Social Services knew nothing about, and the relief she felt was like dark clouds lightening.

"Thank you for saving me," she says as she turns to the edge of the sofa, where nobody is sitting.

But when she closes her eyes, she can imagine Julia there.

"I have some theories," she says. "One of them is that you are an angel."

Angels appear in almost all religions. It means that people have really seen them. Why not one with blond hair, size eight and a half shoes, and a thin little mouth? On the other hand, why would an angel have her make bead mosaic pictures that she didn't know she'd made herself? And, above all, if Julia were an angel, who were those unfocused voices she'd heard when she was a teenager?

"Another theory is that you did exist, but only in my mind. You existed, because you were needed. For everyone else, you were imaginary, but it's like Thor said . . ."

She stops speaking and thinks about Thor's rough hand on Julia's cheek. As he stroked it, he must have been seeing nothing but air. Why did he do this?

"As Thor said, you were in my heart and mind. As real for me as everything else is for everybody else."

A warm body comes and nudges her legs. She opens her eyes and picks up Janus.

"Until I'd healed," she says as she rubs her hand along her dog's back. "Until I no longer wanted to die. So I . . ."

She stops talking. She'd been talking to the wall, with an armchair, with her dog. It suddenly felt ridiculous.

The second thing she did was to choose something she'd been fighting against her entire life.

The thing was, they beat her down, those psychologists. She'd tell them about the voices, the ones who wanted her to cut herself, and they tore her down and never listened. They picked at her until her mind was screaming, *no!* Until her entire being was nothing but one huge *no! Look at me now*, she thinks. *I have a dog, a nice apartment, and a job I figured out by myself. I'm hardly a failure and you know nothing about me.*

She'd made a decision today, a decision she'd never been able to make before. It had not been a choice available to her. Now she picks up her phone. She expects a fight from the voices in her head, but never even feels the urge to put her phone back down.

"Hello, I'd like to make an appointment with a psychologist," she says.

She sounds like an adult.

"I need a specialist on hallucinations and things like that," she explains. "When can I come in for an initial consultation?"

The receptionist asks her if she can wait a few weeks for an appointment or is it more urgent. Pernilla tickles Janus's stomach. Her little dog with the big name.

"I can wait," she says.

It's not acute.

She no longer wants to die.

CHAPTER 43

Kouplan has become a bit bigger since Pernilla first gave him a chicken sandwich. He thinks this as he stands sideways in front of the miniscule bathroom mirror and tries to judge what he looks like. He tenses his arm muscles and thinks his shoulders look wider. Perhaps the constant influx of fish sticks and chicken sausage has played a role.

He now has over nine thousand crowns in cash. It felt odd to take them when he did not actually find Pernilla's child, but she had insisted: *Don't be an idiot.* Nine thousand will be enough for rent, a bus pass, and basic groceries for a few months. That's how he'll divide the money, he thinks, and involuntarily thinks of his debt. He does not want to think of his debt. At least not while he's living on peanuts.

"It's not fair that someone who has terrorized his former partner for years gets off with less punishment than someone who pirated a song on the net," a voice says on the radio.

Astrid Lindgren, the radio, and some people he used to know have taught him all the difficult words. And now he's back to learning. If he is going to keep at this vocation, he needs more words having to deal with crime, and Swedish Radio, luckily enough, has just started a series called *Crime and Punishment*.

"We have to end this debate now," the program leader says for the second time. "We're now going to today's Wanted Criminal."

He's such a vain person, he thinks, remaining hidden and alone and spending time looking at his muscles in a mirror. Then the radio announcer says something that makes him really listen. He's missed the introduction.

"The girl and two women were part of a huge human trafficking ring. The police would like to contact the person who gave them the tip which was delivered through a priest."

"A priest involved in a smuggling ring?" asks the announcer's sidekick.

"No, not the priest . . . a person had called the priest to tip off the police. This person is keeping his identity secret and the priest's duty is to keep his name confidential."

"That was smart!"

The person on the radio was right. It was smart. Kouplan had been thinking about the fact that Thor kept his word even though Kouplan had been hired as Pernilla's private detective. So the priest took his vows seriously, which meant Kouplan could trust him, and Kouplan had his number. So all he had to do was convince Thor of the seriousness of what he had seen. A child who was not a hallucination.

"The police do not believe the tipster had anything to do with the crime, and he or she is not a suspect," the program leader says. The sidekick agrees.

"He or she is just a citizen. A citizen who would not keep silent."

"That's right. So if you are listening, tipster, you can call us here at the radio station. You don't need to give your name. The police would just like to speak to you."

Kouplan almost smiles. The radio personalities are telling more modified truths. *Citizen.* He is definitely not going to call in. But he's glad he made the right decision, for the sake of the child.

The one thing that disturbs Kouplan's vision of his beefier self is the elastic. He checks the window curtains twice before he takes it off. Undoes the metal hooks and lets his chest come free. Tries to ignore the two small bags of fat that others call breasts. He tenses his pectoral muscles and thinks that they've been absorbed a bit more. It's hard to see oneself from the outside. Some evenings he thinks nothing has happened. Others, he thinks he sees the changes. The hormones are worth it. *Don't think about the debt.*

He puts on a T-shirt. He never sleeps without one ever since Liam burst into his room that morning. He turns off the light but doesn't fall asleep. Something is making a light reflection on the ceiling. He focuses on it so that he doesn't have to listen to the confusion in his own head.

He's missing Pernilla. *The mental case,* as she called herself. He misses her. He analyzes this and realizes it's because she needed him. He misses the feeling of being liked, from someone he could touch. But at least he has a bed, he thinks, as his emotions overwhelm him. And nine thousand crowns.

And he is loved, even though he feels no touch. He is loved from a distance. The thought is supposed to calm him and not make him more upset.

"I will think of you every night," his mother had said before he left. "And you must think of me every night."

"I'm thinking of you, *Mâmân,*" he mumbles toward the square of light on the ceiling.

He knows how she prays for them. For him and for his brother Nima. He can hear her voice if he thinks of the words. And if he keeps thinking of the words, he can fall asleep as if he were still a child. Calmly. Happily. As if someone is holding him in a great hand, holding him gently.

> *Allah, let my children live.*
> *Be merciful to them and let them live.*
> *Let them find their way.*
> *Let them be happy.*
> *My brave son Nima.*
> *My wise daughter Nesrine.*

AFTERWORD

This book started with an idea. I'm not going to tell you the idea, in case you're flipping to the back of the book first, as I don't want to give it away. My idea came from the thought of what could happen to a parent who lost their child. There would be a hunt for a kidnapper, but the one who was hired to find the child would come to realize that what was happening was not what he'd first thought. I knew that I needed that detective for my story. Who showed up was not your normal policeman. Instead, a cautious academician appeared, one in difficult circumstances. That was Kouplan. I hadn't written many pages before I realized that his story was greater than a single book.

Where did Kouplan come from? I think he emerged from my life and from situations in which I found myself; the life histories I'd heard and the immigrant students I'd gotten to know as a teacher for Swedish as a Second Language. Most people don't have just a single problem. Problems tend to appear in groups. And reality is even stranger than fiction.

Writing this book would have been more difficult if I hadn't had help from my friends, their friends, and my former students. They shared their experiences: Everything from living with a psychosis, to life in Iran, to the influence of testosterone, to the width of an umbilical cord, to how it feels to be illegal.

Therefore I would like to give my greatest gratitude to all of you, but especially Farzaneh Sohrabi, Shaghayegh Paksima, Shadé Jalali, Zinat Pirzadeh, Nalle Högberg, Linda Carlsson, Valfrid Arvidsson, Oscar Schröder, Mio Olsson, Pouriya, Masoud, and Mehdi, as well as the organizations *Ingen människa är illegal* (IMÄI—No Person Is Illegal) and Stockholm Newcomers.